I LOVE MY INDIA

"I Love My India"

ISBN No: " 978-93-91302-35-1"
1st Edition
Language – English and Hindi

Flairs and Glairs
Publication House
Regd. Under MSME Act.

Disclaimer

This is a work of fiction and solely represent the thoughts of the corresponding authors of the articles. Our editors have tried their best to edit the content of all the authors and check the plagiarism.
All the write-ups in this book are unique and are only published in this book.
In case any plagiarism or error is found, only the author is responsible alone, and not the publisher or the Compilers.

Cover Designing and Book Formatting
Shubham Shah and Ishani Agarwal

Acknowledgement

Special thanks for God who blessed us
and give us supereme power of creativity.Also thanks to all the army man,police and won who fight against enimy Of our country.

Co Authors

Shubham Shha (Founder Flairs and Glairs)
Ishani Agarwal (Co-Founder Flairs and Glairs)
Zala Ramiben Devsibhai (complier)

1. Adity Jitendr
2. Agam Sachdeva
3. Ambuj Kumar
4. Ami Patel
5. Anjna Patel
6. Ankita Nahar
7. Bhavana Maheta
8. Bhola Sheetal
9. Chavda Dipikaben
10. Chhaya Shah
11. Daxa Thakkar
12. Dhiraj Kumar Chaurasiya
13. Divya Ram
14. Divya Rashmi Dudia
15. Ganesh Patil
16. Hetal Chaudhary
17. Himanshu Ravat
18. Ipsita
19. Jadav Manishaben
20. Jaya Bharati Kuntal
21. Jeenal Rathod
22. Jeevitha S.
23. Jyotsnabrn Ravalkajal Sah
24. Kareena Verma
25. Kavita Modi
26. Krishna Motwani
27. Miralben Purohit
28. Mohan Priya K.

29. Mohan Priya S.K
30. Namrata Oza
31. Nilofer Farooqui Tauseef
32. Parul Amit
33. Parmar Rutu
34. Pinky Shah
35. Pravin Patel
36. Pritti Bhatt
37. Rashmi Baweja
38. Sahina Ghugha
39. Sakshee Sharma
40. Saroj Rana
41. Shaimee Oza
42. Shalini B.S.
43. Shivani Joshi
44. Shivangi Suman
45. Shraddha Rai
46. Shristi Rani Panda
47. Subhash Singh Ranjan
48. Urmila Patel
49. Vaibhavi Pandya
50. Vanessa Christian
51. Zarana Raja

Shubham Shah

(Founder- Flairs and Glairs)

Shubham Shah, an entrepreneur at "Flairs & Glairs" a brand with dynamics in events organizing and cultural educational pan INDIA, is a 26yrs old guy who recently has entered the digital platform of imprinting emotions. He has initiated with his own open mic platform to help budding poets and aspiring writers under his brand named as "Teekhe Zasbaaat"

He is a commerce graduate from the Bhagalpur City of Bihar. He states Writing has impersonated him since childhood and he has now been writing for over a decade!

Cooking, on the other hand, is his passion! He also mentions, trying out new things just tickles him!

When asked sir, Why SPICY EMOTIONS?

He smiled and added, "agar jasbaat teekhe na ho toh wo jasbaat kahan" Spices are all that blends! So do his words!

As a chef, he presents to you his dish! Hot and freshly served! Taste it! Feel it! Enjoy it! You can also find his writing in the Book "Teekhe Zasbaaat" and 50+ Co-authored anthologies. With his passion to explore opportunities across Platforms, he is working with keen devotion and We wish him all the very best for his future ventures.

He is Featured in the International Magazine DeMode for his upcoming solo novel.

He is Approved by Ne8x for its Lit Fest, and is a Golden Star Awards 2020 Winner.

He is a India Book of Records Holder for his Anthology Satrang, and has the Grandmaster title by Asia Book of Records, for the same.

He has also been featured in Prabhat Khabar, Dainik Jagran, and a lot of other Newspapers in Bihar for his achievements.

He has been a proud co-author to

India Book Of Records (Title- Black)

World Book Of Records (Title -15 Wonders of Poetries)

India Book Of Records (Title - Aaina)

Vajra World Records Holder (Title - Gustakhi Maaf Hai)

High Range of Records Holder (Title - Gustakhi Maaf Hai)

Indian Book of Records

(Title - Road from Worst to Best)

Share your reviews on his

INSTAGRAM

@spicy_emotions
@shubham4shah

Or via email on

shubham2shah@gmail.com

To stay tuned to his work and opportunities follow his business Handles

INSTAGRAM FACEBOOK YOUTUBE

@flairsandglairs
@teekhezasbaaat

WEBSITE:

https://flairsandglairs.in/
https://flairsandglairs.com/

Ishani Agarwal

(Co-Founder- Flairs and Glairs)

Ishani Agarwal hails from the City of Joy, Kolkata.
She is the co-founder of her Community "Teekhe Zasbaaat" and Flairs and Glairs Publication.
Been a Compiler for 45+ Anthologies, she is in the process for more. Co-authored in 150+ Anthologies. She is a India Book of Records Holder, a Vajra World Records Holder, a High Range of Records Holder, an OMG Book of Records Holder, a Bravo Record holder, a Forever Star Book of World Records and an Indian Book of Records Holder.
Approved by Ne8x for its Lit Fest 2020, and Literary Icon 2020. Also a Golden Star Awards Winner 2020.
She has also been awarded with India Star Republic Award 2021, a part of She Awards by Awards Arc and Winner of Nari Samman 2021 by Literoma.

She is also selected as Best Achiever of the Year by AwardsArc and Most Challenging Compiler Award by Spectrum Awards.
She got her first solo Published,a solo Compilation consisting of first 750 contents of hers, titled "Hand That Burnt While Healing".

She has been featured by the National Magazine "Taree Zameen Par" with the title 'unstoppable'.
Also featured in the International Magazine DeMode for her upcoming solo novel, she is proud to write on social issues, and is happy with the love she is receiving.
Connect with her on Instagram: @Ishani_agarwal_quotes / @compilations_so_far

Zala Ramiben D.Sandeshl
(Complier)

Zala Ramiben A 33Year Old writer. From Veraval ,Gir Somanath. Her workplace at Bharuch District.She Is a Writer and actor . She Loves To Write On Feelings And Emotions Of Human Kind. Government job as teacher.. She got Inspired By The Shreemad Bhagavad Geeta and Sunita William.She is humble lover of Value educational drama.She got many awards from litreture.She got many certificate from Vajra World record,

Book of India and OMG World record as co auther.She published her write up in many news paper,anthology ,magazine and also in book.

She made four solo book and four anthology as complier are ongoing.

सरफरोश

हम हमेशा से एक गीत गुनगुनाते है खास तौर पर तब जब कोई राष्ट्रीय कार्यक्रम हो या फिर और कोई दिन वो गीत है" सरफरोशी की तमन्ना हमारे दिल में है,देखना है जोर कितना कातिल में है"।पर क्या यह गीत का अर्थ भी कोई जानता है क्या?यह गीत का अर्थ है देश के लिए जान देने की तमन्ना।कैसे हम अपनी अंदर की देश प्रति प्रेम को प्रकट कर सकते है?क्या हमे बॉर्डर पर जा कर आंतक वादियों के साथ लड़ाई करनी है या गोलियां खा कर हमारी जान की बाजी लगानी है ?यह काम करने के लिए तो हम सभीको आर्मी में जॉइन होना पड़ेगा।कैसे करे हम यह साबित की हम सच्चे सरफरोश है? चलो इसके बारे में में अपना मंतव्य की छनावट करती हु।

देश के लिए प्रेम हो तो सबसे पहले हमे हमारे परिवार और अडोश पड़ोस वाले के साथ मिलजुल कर रहेना है।परिवार से गांव बनता है,गांव से ही देश बनता है।पहले परिवार प्रति प्यार और दुलार से रहना शीखे।कई लोग है जो परिवार में ठीक से नहीं रहते पड़ोसी से आए दिन झगडा करते है और देश प्रेम की बात करते है।

जब भी गांव या समाजमे कोई कार्य हो तो मिलझुल कर हाथ बटाएं।मा भोम हमे यही सिखाती है एक दूसरे को सहारा दो,एक दूसरे के साथ लड़ाई मत करो सहयोग से रहो।चाहो परस्पर एकदुझे को, साहो परस्पर एकदुझे को। साहो माना मदद करो।

अपने घर, आंगन ,गली, महोल्ला,गांव,गांव की सारे वो स्थल जो जाहिर मिलकत में आए स्वच्छ रखो,गांव में कम्पोस्ट खड्डा बनाओ,घर पर कचरा पेटी रखो जब भर जाए तब कम्पोस्ट खड्डे में ही डाले।अगर कभी बस स्टैंड पर जाओ या रेलवे स्टैंड जाओ वहा की स्वच्छता का पूरा ख्याल रखो।अगर अपने देश प्रति प्यार है तो जंहा तंहा थूकना मत,जंहा तंहा कचरा न फेंके।अगर देश प्रति प्यार है तो मा धरा को गंदी मत बनाओ।जहा भी जाओ प्लास्टिक का उपयोग करना टाल दिया करो।आप जिस कार्यक्षेत्र में हो उस कार्यक्षेत्र में अपना कार्य सम्पूर्ण निष्ठा से निभाओ। कीसी भी कार्य में वेठ मत करो।सम्पूर्ण

निष्ठा और लगन से अपना कार्य निभाना यह भी देश प्रति प्रेम का एक लक्षण है।बस यूं ही अपने आप को सरफरोशी बनाओ।

बापू को नमन

कोटि-कोटि नमन बापू को कोटि-कोटि नमन।
करे हृदय से अर्पण श्रद्धा सुमन।।
कताई करके चरखे से कपड़े जिस ने बनाये।
एक उन्माद में जीवन जीसने बिताया।।
ऐसे मेरे बापु को कोटि-कोटि नमन ।।
तीन बंदर का खिलोना बनाया।
सदाचार का मार्ग बताया।
स्वदेशी अपनाओ का संदेशा फैलाया।।
ऐसे मेरे बापु को कोटि-कोटि नमन ।।
अहिंसा के मार्ग पर अंग्रेजों को भगाया।
आराम हराम है सूत्र अपनाया।
स्वच्छता अभियान का पाठ सिखाया।।
ऐसे मेरे बापु को कोटि-कोटि नमन ।।
मेरे बापू मुझे प्राणों से भी प्यारे है।
विचार उनके सारे जग से न्यारे है।।
गांधी तेरा अमर इतिहास है।
याद तेरी श्वासोश्वास है।।

शोर्ट एवं स्वीट।

चलो सच्ची रिती से गांधीजयंती मनाते हैं
करते हैं जीवन में ग्रहण गांधीजी के कुछ विचारों को
बनाते हैं फिर से रामराज्य इस भारत देश को।।

Adity Jitendr

He is Adity kumar Jitendbhai Vasava from primary school pathar.He study in std 7.He write his write up with Nick name Adi.He published his write up in two anthology.He is very clever boy.

હું દેશ માટે કરીશ......

હું અત્યારે ખૂબ જ નાનો છે.પણ અત્યારે જે દેશમાં હું રહ્યુ છું એના પર ગર્વ કરું છું.હું ધોરણ 7 મા અભ્યાસ કરું છું.અમારે રોજ પ્રાર્થનામાં પ્રતિજ્ઞાપત્ર બોલાવે.એમાં કહે હુ મારા દેશને ચાહું છું.ટીચર કહે જેને આપણે પ્રેમ કરીએ એના માટે આપણે કંઈ પણ કરી શકીએ.તો આજે હું દેશ માટે શું કરવાનું મારું સપનું છે એ જણાવીશ.મારા દેશ માટે હું અત્યારે તો મહેનત કરીને ભણું છું ,તો જ કમાઈશ કે કૈંક આવડત હશે તો દેશને આપી શકીશ.શાળા બંધ છે પણ રોજ એમ એસ ટીમ મા જોડાઈ ભણું છું.મારા ગલી મા ક્યાંય કચરો ન હોય એનું ધ્યાન રાખું છું .મે તો એકવાર પપ્પાને કંપોસ્ટ ખાડો પણ ખોદવા કહ્યું.ગંદકી હોય તો આપણે બીમાર પડીએ અને આપણું મન બગડે એટલે ભણી ન શકીએ ,કઈ કરી ન શકીએ તો દેશની સેવા કઈ રીતે કરવાના?

મોટો થઈશ એટલે મારા દેશ માટે બધા સાથે વાત કરી આખા ગામમાં બધી જ સુવિધા કરાવીશ.ચોખ્ખું પાણી,પાકા રસ્તા અને ઘેર ઘેર કચરા પેટી ,દૂર એક કમ્પોસ્ટ ખાડો.ઘરે ઘરે સૌચાલય...નવી સ્કૂલની માંગ પણ કરીશ જેમ કે અમારા ગામ થી એક કિલોમીટર દૂર ચાલી નાના નાના છોકરાઓ આવે ....છોકરાઓને શૈક્ષણિક કીટ જેમાં પેન્સીલ,પેન,નોટ,રૂમાલ વગેરે હોય સાથે બુટ મોજા સ્વેટર હોય આ બધું હું મોટી મોટી કંપનીમાં જઈને આપવા સમજાવીશ.ઝૂંપડ પટ્ટી દૂર કરાવી નાના મકાન બનાવડાવીશ.ઘરે ઘરે ગેસ ની સુવિધા થાય એ માટે કોઈક દ્વારા સરકારમાં કહેવડાવીશ.જે ગામ,મહોલ્લો,વૃક્ષ વગરનો હશે ત્યાં

અમારું ગૃપ બનાવી મહોલ્લે મહોલ્લે ફરી વૃક્ષારોપણ કરીશું. મોંઘવારી ને લીધે ગરીબ લોકોને ભૂખ્યા રહેવું પડે અને ક્યારેક મરી પણ જાય તો હું સૌથી પહેલો પ્રયત્ન મોંઘવારી દૂર કરવાનો કરીશ.પ્રયત્ન કરીશ કે દરેક ગામમાં એક સરકારી દવાખાનું હોય એમાં પાછા બધા પ્રકારના રોગ સારા થતાં હોય.કેમ કે કોઈ દવા ન હોવાથી મરે નહિ.અમારા ગામ બાજુ ને ઘણા ગામ માં ભૂવા ને માને,સાપ કરડે તો પણ ભૂવા પાસે જાય દવાખાને નહી એથી કોઈક દિવસ લોકો મરી જાય.હું મોટો થઈશ તો ગામના મહોલ્લાઓમાં રેલી કાઢી બધાને વિજ્ઞાનનું મહત્વ સમજાવીશ.આ માટે અત્યારથી હુ બધી સ્પર્ધામાં ભાગ લઉં.એટલે મને કોઈ સાથે વ્યવસ્થિત બોલવાનું આવડે અને હું મારા દેશની સેવા કરી શકું.

Agam Sachdeva

She is an extremely talented girl with a very beautiful mind. She is 14 years old and at such young age touching up those skies. She has made her parents really proud.

Independence Day

Freedom has a high cost,
Lives given the ultimate loss,
That cost they willingly give,
So freedom can continue to live.
15 August 1947, the day we got freedom,
Was us, standing a bright nation as one.
All the freedom which we earned, that gave us happiness and the independence.

Today we come together and unite, and we don't have any other good day and either and schools gift us a little donut. The day is very special and year by year, it became more crucial.

Republic Day

We Indians are very proud to celebrate Republic Day,
Protected by soldiers on the border who never sway,
Hear me, I have few things to say,
Reading this you may decide your own way.

Over the years that has past,
26 Jan is just another holiday", I thought,
ith the very recent wisdom I have got,
I salute the leaders ago has fought.
I hear the media " flash news"
And end up in tear "will there be more bomb blasts?" I fear.
The pride of Indians in atmosphere and devotion of the nation in my heart, lies here.

Ambuj Kumar

Name -Ambuj Kumar
He is a teacher
He belobngs to Sanahpur Darbhanga
His hobby is writing

मेरा प्यारा हिंदुस्तान

होली की रंगोली
बंगाल की दुर्गामहरानी
मेरा प्यारा हिंदुस्तान

गणपति पपा मोर्या मराठी की
अयोध्या बनी राम की
मेरा प्यारा हिंदुस्तान

किसान की हरियाली
गेहुँ की खेत लहलहाती
मेरा प्यारा हिंदुस्तान

सात रंगों से रंगोली बनायी
मिथिला जैसी जिला बनायी
मधुबनी ने दुनिया को कला सिखायी
मेरा प्यारा हिंदुस्तान

करोना जैसी महामारी
संसार को शिकार बनाया शिकारी
फिर भी भारत बना सबसे भारी
मेरा प्यारा हिंदुस्तान

धरती फटी घड़ा फुटी
मिथिला धरती को पवित्र बनाई
मेरा प्यारा हिंदुस्तान

सामाजिक रूप से सुद्दढ़ बनायी
5 साल की मिसाल बनायी
देश को चाँद की शिखर पर लायी
मेरा प्यारा हिंदुस्तान

मेरा प्यारा हिंदुस्तान

किसानों को महत्व देने वाला
पिछडो़ को योजनाओं देने वाला
मेरा प्यारा हिंदुस्तान

सेना को हौसला बढ़ाने वाला
सरहद को बचाने वाला
मेरा प्यारा हिंदुस्तान

56 इंच का सीना रखने वाला
योगी जैसे कलेजा रखने वाला
मेरा प्यारा हिंदुस्तान

धर्मो मे ना भेद-भाव रखनेवाला
अनेकता मे एकता भाव रखने वाला
मेरा प्यारा हिंदुस्तान

शिक्षा मे समानता लाने वाला
रोटी- कपड़ा और मकान-दुकान
मेरा प्यारा हिंदुस्तान

रोजगार – समाचार दिलाने वाला
नल- जल घर-घर पहुंचाने वाला
मेरा प्यारा हिंदुस्तान

Ami Patel

She is Ami Patel .She is Writer, poet and explorer .She write her write up in
Many anthologies.

Country Is Always First

Niranjan was shocked. Life had shown him a very unfair side. He couldn't move from his place. His body was frozen. He heard his father speaking to the commissioner of police on the telephone.

"Kill him otherwise we will be finished." Said his father.

"But he has already spoken about it to our superiors, Mr. Desai." Spoke commissioner from the other side of the phone. Niranjan was listening to the conversation from his room by another connected landline of the house. He couldn't believe his ears. It was hard for him to grasp that his father wanted to kill someone.

"Kill them all. In return I will give you whatever you want. Just do what I say. Find out a number of people who know this in your department and kill all of them."

"Are you sure?"

"Yes, Kill that informer first and then others. Plan it in a way that it look like terrorist attack."

Niranjan was a 'flying officer' in Indian Air Force. His father was one of the top businessman of India. He wanted his only son to become the biggest businessman of the world but Niranjan had his mother's brain in his body. Money was nothing for him. He wanted to serve his motherland. After so much struggle, he was finally granted permission from his father to go ahead with his chosen career.

He was there on a one month leave. His father was in tension for two-three days and he was aware of that. He couldn't decide what to do in this situation but after some time he gained that confidence. After all, he was trained by one of the best 'flight lieutenant' of Indian Air Force.

He called his superior. He talked to him and then moved down stairs. He entered his father's room and stood at a stone's throw away from him. Was his father doing it to save innocent people? Or himself? Was he involved in any scam? Was he protecting someone from those people? Niranjan had many questions in his head and he wanted his father to confront him so that he and his superior could decide what to do next. He was sure that his father would not harm him.

"I heard everything dad." He said.

"What?" His father Mr. Desai startled.

"Your telephonic conversation with the commissioner."

"It's nothing son. It is just a part of businessmen's routine. Don't worry. It is problematic but I will handle it."

"Killing people is part of your routine? I want to know everything dad. Please tell me." Niranjan screamed.

"Actually our company got a tender of building a smart city near Pune. I want to develop it specially for tourism. We planned everything but at the last time some farmers who were leaving there, changed their mind and protested to get their land back from the government. They even denied the proposal of our company in which we were offering them a job and a huge security amount."

"Then?"

"Government was thinking to fulfil their demand and cancel the tender. Our company had already invested a lot in that

Anjana Patel

She is Anjana Ben Patel from Ahemdabad.She is an innovative teacher at Sanskartirth Ajol.She is principal at there.Her hobbies are anchoring,writing and reading.She also selected in state level virtual class teacher.She is state level winner in toy fair and innovation fair .

देश को बचाना है
जन जन का यह नारा है ।
कोरोना से देश को बचाना है।।
हमे नियमों का पालन करना है।
कोरोना के देश से भगाना है।
हाथ मिलाने से हमे बचना है ।
नमस्ते से अपने पुरखों को याद करना है।।
हमे सामाजिक अंतर रखना है।
कोरोना से खुद को बचाना है।।
कोरोना वारियर्स का
सम्मान हमे करना है।
कर कुछ न सके ना कोई बात है हमे हिमत किसीकी बढ़ाना है।।
हम सबका यही विश्वास है।
वो महामारी है तो
हम भी आखिर इंसान है।।
करते है सलाम सफाई कामदारो को।
पहले करते सड़क की सफाई फिर जाते अपने घर।।
ऐसे होगे जब इस देश में ।
तब तो ऊंचा उठेगा देश का सर।।
ये देश को गरीब ही चलाएगा।
कोई काम को न माने जो छोटा,
अपने कंधे पर सारी जिमेदारी ले लेता।।
आज डॉक्टर,नर्स,पुलिस ,शिक्षक ,मीडिया,सरकार कोरोना से लड़ते है।
उन सब को सहना है ,
हमे सिर्फ नियम का पालन करना है।।
हिंदुस्तानी है हम
हमे इतिहास याद करना है।
बापू,भगतसिंह ,सुखदेव ने भगाया अंग्रेजो को,हमे कोरोना को भगाना है।।

हमे नियम में रहकर
योद्धा के हौसले को
बढ़ाना है।
कोरोना को भगाने में
कामयाब एक दिन होना है।।
हमे अपने देश को बचाना है।
देशप्रेम को हमे अब जताना है।।
स्वच्छता से खुद को सुरक्षित रखना है।
सुरक्षित रहकर देश को बचाना है।।
आओ बच्चो ,आओ यूवाओ ले शपथ ।
बढ़ाते है आगे कोरोना वॉरियर्स का रथ।।

Ankita Nahar

Ankita Nahar, physically she live in Rajasthan but heartly live in everywhere.

She is too much passionate about writing.

She have always found comfort in words, and that's what attracts everyone.Writing is her therapy, she write what she feels and experiences in her life. You can take a look at her writings on Instagram @naharankita1

आजादी

सुना हैं अच्छी चीजो को बनने ने समय लगता है
वैसे ही समय लगा था भारत के संविधान में
समय लगा था भारत की आजादी में
समय लगा था भारत को भारत बनने में
और ना जाने क्या क्या लगा था
२६ जनवरी को गणतंत्र दिवस बनने में
ना जानें कितने लोग वीरगति को प्राप्त हुए
ना जाने कितनो के सिंदूर और कितनी माओं की कोख़ आजादी में काम आयी
आज भी याद हैं मुझे
मां अक्सर सुनाया करती हैं
भगतसिंह का बलिदान,
पद्मावती का जौहर
शिवाजी, रानी लक्ष्मीबाई
और ना जाने कितने ही वीरों
की कहानियां
मैं बात करूं उन वीरांगनओं की
इतने शब्द मेरे पास हैं नहीं
बस इतना ही कहूंगी की
मौत तुझसे बहुत ज्यादा सिफारिश नहीं हैं
बस जब भी तू आए
तब ऐसी आये की
सिर पर कफ़न नहीं तिरंगा हो ।

Bhavna Maheta

She is presently pursuing B.Ed from Guru Jambheshwar University, Hisar.She lives in small town, Bhuna.She like to pen down her thoughts.She has written two Blogs and won Blog Competition also.She has interest in other activities also.She has won District Level Debate Competition, Dance Competition and Photography Competition also.

मेरा भारत महान-
चार ऋतुओं का आगमन होता हैं जहां,
सात नदियों का संगम हैं जहां,
हर त्योहार का अपना अंदाज हैं जहां,
ये मेरा भारत हैं महान।
धरती में जहां सोना उगता,
खाने में हैं अनेक पकवान,
कोई फौजी तो कोई हैं विद्वान,
ये मेरा भारत हैं महान।
सब रहते यहां मिल-जुलकर,
प्यार बांटते हर जगह,
ये मेरा भारत हैं महान।।

Bhola Sheetal

She is Bhola sheetal Ben virabhai from sutrapada Gir Somnath.She study in std 11th in kanya vinay mandir Ajol.She write many article and try to write drama.

રાષ્ટ્રપ્રેમ.....? વાસ્તવ માં રાષ્ટ્રપ્રેમ એટલે શું?અન્ય દેશની સરખામણી મા પોતાના દેશની બડાઈ કરવી તે...? ના ના...ના.....ચાલો આજે રાષ્ટ્રપ્રેમ વિશે મારા વિચારો સમજાવુ.

રાષ્ટ્ર પ્રેમ એટલે જ્યાં અન્યાય થતો હોય ત્યાં પોતાનું સર્વસ્વ રેડી અન્યાયનો સામનો કરવો,જેને અન્ન વસ્ત્ર આદી ન મળતું હોય પોતાની જરૂરિયાતના ભોગે અન્ન વસ્ત્ર પૂરા પાડવા,પોતાનો અમૂલ્ય સમય આપી દિન દુખિયાની સેવા કરવી. મુશ્કેલી ના સમયમાં પ્રાણ ના ભોગે પણ અન્યને બચાવવા.તમામ બાબતમાં સાચો રાષ્ટ્રપ્રેમ સમાયેલ છે. અતિશયોક્તિ ન થતી હોય તો હું તો ત્યાં સુધી કહીશ કે આવો રાષ્ટ્રપ્રેમ જ ઈશ્વર સુધી પહોંચવાનો માર્ગ છે.

આપણે યાદ કરીએ ભારતના જશવંત સિંહ રાવતને જેણે 72 કલાક ચીન સામે લડીને પોતાના જીવનના બલિદાન દ્વારા અરુણાચલ પ્રદેશ ની ભૂમિ ને બચાવી લીધી.એકલા હાથે આ કઈ રીતે શક્ય બન્યું ,કારણ કે તે અન્યાય સામે લડતો હતો.તેની અંદર રાષ્ટ્રપ્રેમ હતો.

આપણા દેશના અનેક વીરોએ અને સંતોએ પોતાના જીવનનું બલિદાન આપી અજ્ઞાની ભારત,ગરીબ ભારત, કંગાળ ભારતવાસીની સેવા કરી છે.ભારત દેશને વિકસિત બનાવવામાં પોતાનું યોગદાન આપેલ છે.આવા શબ્દો ઉચ્ચારતા ઝાંસીની રાણી,ભગતસિંહ,ગાંધીજી,સરદાર યાદ આવી જાય ને....

દરેક ભારતવાસીઓને ગર્વ થવો જોઇએ કે આપણો સ્ત્રીત્વ નો આદર્શ સીતા અને સાવિત્રી છે.ભૂલવાનું નથી કે આપણા ઉપાસ્ય દેવ શંકર સર્વસ્વ ત્યાગી છે.આ શરીર આપણા સુખ માટે નથી દેશના હિત માટે છે.

Chavada Dipika Ben

वह दीपिका बहन चावड़ा गुजरात से है।वह एक रिटायर्ड शिक्षक है।गांधीजी के बारे में,हमारे इतिहास के बारे में कई सारे नाटक उसने बच्चो को तैयार करवाए है।वो बहुत होनहार लेखिका है।

देशप्रेमी

हमारी सुरक्षा के लिए देश की सरहद पर दिन रात अहर्नीश कार्य करने वाले हमारी भारतीय सेना पर हमे बहुत गर्व है। सेना में सैनिक अपने जीव को जोखिम में डालकर हमारे देश की सुरक्षा के लिए लड़ते है और अपनी निष्ठा एवं कर्तव्य पालना की भावना को उजागर करते करते हमारे देश को दुश्मनों से सुरक्षित और स्वतंत्र रखते है।

हमारे भारत के संविधान में

अनिवार्य भर्ती का उल्लेख हुआ है लेकिन उनके अमल की जरूरत ही नहीं पड़ी क्योंकि आज भी भारत की हर सेना का सैनिक अपनी ख़ुशी से देश के लिए लड़ने के लिए तैयार होता है यह गर्व की बात है।

आज ईस तरह के एक सैनिक की यहां बात करना चाहूंगी।

बहुत समय पहले की बात है। भारत का ही एक अंतरियाल छोटे गांव का युवान। उनको अपने देश पर बहुत प्यार और गौरव था। यही प्यार को उजागर करने के लिए वो युवान लश्कर में दाखिल हुआ था। उसकी देश के लिए कुछ भी कर छूटने की तैयारी,कार्य प्रति धगश के कारण ऊपरी अधिकारी उनसे बहुत प्रभावित थे ।

एक बार देश के ऊपर दुश्मन देश के सैन्य ने हमला किया और सरहद पर युद्ध शुरू हुआ।सारे सैनिकों का यह युद्धमे देश की रक्षा के लिए उत्साह से सामिल हुए। यह युवक भी उस युद्ध में सामिल हुआ। दुश्मनों के सामने खंत से लड़कर दुश्मनों को हराकर जीत हासिल की।देशमे खुशियों का माहौल छा गया।सारे देशवासी जीत की खुशियां मनाने में लग गए लेकिन कुछ सैनिक इस युद्ध में शहीद हुए और कई सैनिकों को दुश्मन देश कैदी बनाकर ले गए।

यह देशप्रेमी युवक भी कैदी बन कर और दुश्मनदेश की कैद में गए।बरसो के बाद अपने देश में से किसीको इन सैनिकों की याद न आईं।अपनी प्रमाणिकता के कारण इस युवक को छोड़ दिया गया।वो

अपने देश परत आया लेकिन किसीने उनकी नोंध नहीं ली और न तो किसीने उनकी मदद की।
अपने हुन्नर के बल पर इस युवान को प्राइवेट कम्पनी में नोकरी मिली और बहुत कम सेलरी में अपने घर के लोगो का भरण पोषण कर रहे थे।
उसने दी गई देशप्रेम की आहुति   समय के प्रवाह में चली गई। आज इतने कई देशप्रेमी है जिसके परिवार की कोई ऑथ नहीं।
आज इस पुस्तक की माध्यम से गुजारिश करती हु की जिस देशप्रेमी के कारण हम अपने घर में चैन की नींद सो रहे है उनको भी याद किया जाए।

Chhaya Shah

She is Chhayaben Jayeshbhai Shah from Mumbai.She write her write up with Nick name sakhy.She is also a editor.She write many type of literature like article story poem drama etc.Her native place is kucchh from Gujrat.

સદગુણ થી દેશસેવા
નીરા આર્યા –

નારી ધારે તો શું ન કરી શકે?એમાં પણ જો દેશપ્રેમની ભાવના હોય તો તો વાત જ શું પૂછવી.મનની મક્કમતા ,દ્રઢ નિશ્ચય,હિંમત અને આ સમગ્ર દેશ મારો સ્વજન છે એને હાની પહોચાડનાર ને ક્યારેય ન છોડે પછી ભલે તે આપણા લૌકિક પરિવારમાંથી પણ ભલે હોય એવી ભાવનાનું શ્રેષ્ઠ ઉદાહરણ એટલે નીરા આર્યા જે દેશની પહેલી મહિલા જાસૂસી રહી ચૂકી છે. નીરા આર્યાનો જન્મ 5 માર્ચ 1902 નાં હમણાં ના ઉત્તરપ્રદેશનું ખેકડા નામનાં શહેરમાં થયું હતું. એનાં પિતા એક વેપારી હતાં. એનો વ્યાપાર દેશભરમાં ફેલાયો હતો. વ્યાપારનું મુખ્ય કેન્દ્ર કોલક્તા હોવાથી નારી શિક્ષણ કોલકતામાં થયું હતુ. નારી આર્યા હિન્દી, અંગ્રેજી, બંગાળી સાથે સાથે બીજી પણ કેટલીક ભાષાઓ જાણતાં હતાં. એમનાં લગ્ન બ્રિટિશ ભારતનાં cid ઇન્સ્પેક્ટર શ્રીકાંત જયરંજન દાસ સાથે થઈ હતી. અંગ્રેજ અધિકારી હતાં. શ્રીકાંત અને સુભાષચંદ્ર બોઝની જાસૂસી ને મારવાની જિમ્મેદારી સોંપવામાં આવી હતી.

નિરા આર્યએ નેતાજી સુભાષચંદ્ર બોઝની જાન બચાવવા માટે અંગ્રેજ સભામાં અફસર, પોતાનાં પતિ શ્રીકાંત રંજન દાસની હત્યા કરી નાખી હતી. અવસર જોઈને શ્રીકાંતે નેતાજીને મારવા ગોળીઓ ચલાવી. એ ગોળીઓ નેતાજીનાં ડ્રાઇવરને લાગી, પરંતુ એ દરમિયાન નીરા આર્યા શ્રીકાંતનાં પેટમાં સંગીન (ચાકુ,

કટાર)થી વાર કરીને પોતાના પતિને મોતને ઘાટ ઉતારી દીધાં હતાં. શ્રીકાંત નીરા આર્યાનાં પતિ હતાં, એટલે પતિને મારવાનાં કારણથી જ નેતાજીએ એમને 'નાગીન' ઉપનામ આપ્યું અને પછી એઓ નીરા નાગીનનાં નામથી પ્રખ્યાત થયાં.

ભારતના સ્વાતંત્ર સંગ્રામમાં એમનું મહત્વનું યોગદાન હતુ. નીરા આર્યા ત્યારે (1902 - 1998) આઝાદ હિંદ ફોજમાં રાની ઝાંસી રેજીમેન્ટનાં સિપાહી હતાં જેમનાં પણ અંગ્રેજ સરકારે ગુપ્તચર હોવાનો આરોપ પણ લગાવ્યો હતો.

નીરા આર્યા એક મહાન દેશભક્ત, સાહસી અને સ્વભાવનાં હતાં. નીરા આર્યાનાં નામ પર રાષ્ટ્રીય પુરસ્કાર પણ છે. એમને ગર્વ અને ગૌરવ સાથે યાદ કરવામાં આવે છે.

આ લેખ લખવાનું કારણ એટલું જ કે રાષ્ટ્રપ્રેમની ભાવના માટે ભારતની તમામ નારીની અંદર આ ગુણો હોવા અત્યંત જરૂરી છે.સમગ્ર દેશને પોતાનો માની દેશને નુકશાન પહોંચાડનાર ભલે તે પોતાનો પુત્ર હોય ,પતી હોય કે અન્ય કોઈ સ્વજન હંમેશા મન મક્કમ રાખી એને પાઠ ભણાવી દરેક નારી રાષ્ટ્ર માટે પોતાનું યોગદાન આપે એ જરૂરી છે.

કહેવાય છે ને કે **charity begins from home.** દરેક નારી પોતાના પરિવારમાં ગુનાહિત પ્રવૃત્તિ અટકાવશે તો દેશ આપોઆપ ગુનારહિત બની જશે.

Daxaben Thakkar

She is Daxaben Thakkar .She is retired from L.I.C.Her hobbies are writing and reading.She won fifty eight poem contest.She got many madal and certificate from literature like Namaskar Gujrat,Virat hindi sahity yuva munch.She got many trophies and books in literature…

आझादी.....

कितनी मुश्किल से पाई है,
पाई है हमने आजादी।
बापू अगर न होते तुम
लकडी के टेक न आते तुम।
उपवास का शस्त्र था आपका,
और खून था कर्म वीरों का।

किमत बडी चुकाई सबने,
जान दी है उन क्रांतिकारीयोंने।

भगत,,राज,,सुखदेव,,सुभाष की,
बलि चढी है पाने आजादी।

खूब लडी मर्दानी अपनी,
कमाल झांसी की रानी।

अंग्रेजो से खूब लडी,
रौंदा घोडों के पैरों तले।

तात्या,,नाना,,नैनावती,
प्रताप और वीर सावरकर,

बापट,,, गोखले,,,रानाडे और,
अनेक अनगिनत क्रांतिकारी, ने

धूल चटाई है दुश्मनों को
कुर्बानी दी,,,देश के लिये।

गुरु गोविन्द ,,,, परिवार सहित,
हुए न्योछावर आजादी के लिये।

सभी क्रांतिवीरों के खून से ,
छबी बनी मां भारती की।

आज हम जो सांस ले रहे,
आजाद भूमि भारत में ,

कुर्बानी दी है वीर सपूतों ने ,
ना भूले है, ना भूलेगे।

दक्षा ठाकर,, 'दक्षु'

Dhirajkumar Saurachiya

Name -Dhiraj kumar chaurasia
He is 21 years old .
He is the student of graduation
He is from Sanahpur (Bihar)
He is the co -author of many Books .
His hobby is writing and reading .
Fb handle/- Dhiraj kumar chaurasia
Insta- Dhirajchaurasi57

हिंदुस्तान

ये फूलों की खुश्बू
ये गांवों की सड़कें
बड़ा निराला है ये नज़ारा हिंदुस्तान का ।

ये बादलें
ये हवाएं
यूँ झमक कर बरसना
बड़ा सुहाना लगता है
मौसम हिंदुस्तान का ।

प्यार -मोहब्बत
अमन- परस्ती
सब संस्कार है हिंदुस्तान का ।

ये विरो की गाथा
ये शहिदो कहानी
बड़ा निराला है कि कहानी हिंदुस्तान का ।

सब देशों से प्यार
है ये देश हमारा
बच्चा बच्चा बोले हिंदुस्तान का ।
हां ये नज़ारा बड़ा निराला है हिंदुस्तान का ।।
सबसे सुंदर सबसे प्यारा
ये देश हमारा ।

हिन्दू- मुस्लिम हो
या हो सिख ईसाई
कहलाते सब भाई भाई ।

ना बैर है लोगों में
ना सड़को पर मनमौजी है
ये देश है वीर जवानों का
हर घर से एक फौजी है ।

ये देश है सबसे प्यारा
हिंदुस्तान जान हमारा है ।

Divyaben Ram

She is Ram Divya Ben Dineshbhai.She is housewife and write her write up in online mode like pratilipi.She pulished her write up in many anthology.Her hobbies are reading writing and sports.She is hard working women.

દેશપ્રેમ

" દેશ મેરા મેરી જાન હે તું "
દેશ મેરે દેશ મેરે મેરી શાન હે તું"

એવો મારો ભારત દેશ બધા દેશો કરતાં પણ વધારે સુંદર છે.આખી દુનિયા માં ભારત જેવો કોઈ દેશ નથી અહીંયા અનેક જાત ના લોકો વસે છે અહી અનેક ભાષા બોલાય છે તો વળી જુદા જુદા તહેવારો પણ ઉજવાય છે આપણા દેશ મા ભલે જુદી જુદી જાતીના લોકો વસતા હોય પણ બધા સાથે હળી મળી ને રહે છે અહી હિન્દુ ઈદ તો મુસ્લિમ દિવાળી ઉજવી રહ્યા છે.અહીંયા ગણેશ ચતુર્થી પણ મનાવાય છે ને નાતાલ પણ... એવો દેશ છે આપણો. આપણા મન માં દેશભક્તિ ની ભાવના તો હોવી જ જોઈએ જે આપણા દેશ માં છે એ બીજે ક્યાંય નથી .આપણા દેશ ને આઝાદ કરવા માટે ઘણા દેશભક્તો એ પોતાનું બલિદાન આપ્યું . આપણા દેશ ના વીર જવાનો એ પોતાના જીવ ની પરવાહ કર્યા વિના દેશ ને આઝાદ કરવા અનેક આંદોલન અને અનેક લડાઈઓ કરી હતી ત્યારે આપણે આઝાદી મળી હતી અને ત્યારે જ આજે આપણે સ્વતંત્ર જીવી રહ્યા છે પરંતુ ધીરે ધીરે આપણી આવનારી પેઢી આ બધું ભૂલતી જાય છે અને પાછી એ સંસ્કૃતિ તરફ વળવા લાગી છે જેને છોડાવવા આપણા પૂર્વજો લડ્યા હતા આજે તો દેશભક્તિ ને નામે રાજનીતિ રમાઈ રહી છે ,આંદોલન ને નામે ગરીબ પ્રજા ને મારી રહ્યા છે. આજે આપણા ભારત માં જ્યાં હળી મળી ને તહેવારો ઉજવાતા

ત્યાં આજે કોમી રમખાણો ની રાજનીતિ રમાડી ભાઈ ભાઈ ઝઘડી રહ્યા છે પેલા આપણો દેશ સોનાની ચીડિયા માનવામાં આવતો હતો એજ દેશ ને દેશ ના રાજનીતિ વાળા એ કર્જમાં ડુબાડી દીધો.

આપણે શું કરી શકીએ આમાં....?આખો પરિવાર હળી મળીને રહી શકીએ.પરિવારની એકતા થી ગામની ,શહેરની અને દેશની એકતા વધે છે. આપણે સૌથી પહેલા માનવ ધર્મ નિભાવવો જોઈએ.એનાથી જ દેશની પ્રજા વિકસિત બનશે. આપણે આપણા ઘર ,મહોલ્લા વગેરે ને સ્વચ્છ રાખી આપણા દેશને સ્વચ્છ ,સ્વસ્થ રાખી આપણી બૌધિક શક્તિ નો દેશને આપી દેશને આગળ વધારવા પ્રયત્ન કરવો જોઈએ .રોજગાર માટે નહિ, આપણી ઇજ્જત માટે નહિ પણ દેશના વિકાસ માટે આપણે હોનહાર બનવું જોઈએ. આપણે આપણી આવડતને વધારવી અને એનો ઉપયોગ આપણા દેશના

વિકાસ માટે કરવો જોઇએ. આપણે ગામ લોકોએ હળી મળીને રહેવું જોઈએ. જો આપણી આસપાસ

ગંદકી હશે તો આપણું મન અને શરીર સ્વસ્થ નહિ રહે અને અસ્વસ્થ મન અને અસ્વસ્થ શરીર

સાથે આપણે આપણી આવડતને વિકસિત નહિ કરી શકીએ અને રાષ્ટ્રના વિકાસમાં આપણે

આપણું યોગ્ય યોગદાન ન આપી શકીએ. આપણે આપણી આસપાસ થતાં ભ્રષ્ટાચારને

રોકવો જોઈએ અને ભ્રષ્ટાચાર મુક્ત ભારત બનાવવામાં આપણું

શ્રેષ્ઠ યોગદાન આપવું જોઈએ. આપણે આપણા દેશમાં વિકાસના કાર્યો થાય એ માટે મર્યાદામાં રહેવું જોઈએ.પુરુષો e સ્ત્રીઓનું ધ્યાન રાખવું જોઈએ.

સૌથી મોટી વાત આપણે બ્યુટી પાર્લર માં જવાને બદલે ચણાનો લોટ,મધ,લીંબુ વગેરેથી આપણું કુદરતી સૌંદર્ય વધારી રાષ્ટ્ર પ્રત્યે પ્રેમ જતાવવો જોઈએ.વિદેશી ઠંડા પીણા ને બદલે નારિયેળ પાણી અને શેરડીનો રસ પી તૃપ્ત થઇ.આ રીતે વિદેશી વસ્તુનો બહિષ્કાર કરી સ્વદેશી અપનાવી દેશભક્તિનું ઉત્તમ ઉદાહરણ પૂરું પાડીએ.....

Divya Rashmi Dudia

Divya Rashmi Dudia hails in Jodhpur Rajasthan and is a financial anaylst.She loves to learn new skills and is epistemophile when comes to knowledge.She is into writing since last two years and has been a part of few anthologies and loves to read a lot .She is a nature lover and loves to help people around her .She believes in spreading smiles and motivation.

देशभक्ति#

उठ जाग देश बुला रहा
है तू उसकी संतान आज वो बुला रहा
खुद से पहले उसको दे उसको तव्वजो क्योंकि तू जन्मा है उसमें
फख्र कर तू है हिंदुस्तानी है उस देश में जहां है बहुत से राजधानी
बहुत सी संस्कृति के लोग आते है साथ
हिंदू ,मुस्लिम ,सिख हिसाई सब यहां है भाई भाई
क्या गुजरती,मराठी, सिंधी,मारवाड़ी सब भाषाएं है बहुत प्यारी
एक दूसरे के त्यौहार और संस्कृति को अपनाते है जहां सब
करते है मदद हर पल चाहे कहीं भी हो संस्कार नहीं भूलते है हम
सहजता ,आदर ,सम्मान,एक दूसरे की मदद करना यही है हर
भारतीय का काम
गर्व करो की हम यहां जन्मे और मातृभूमि के लिए कुछ कर जाए
हम है हिंदी अपना फर्ज़ निभा पाए ।

#India#

The culture that is full of colours
The culture which has unity in diversity
The culture which taught us to respect each religion
We are indians
We are proud hindustani
The beauty of it is to be treasured
The heritage of it is to be treasured
We have such unsung heros
We have such unsung sheros do your part and make the
world proud
Respect it and keep loving india .

Ganesh Patil

This Is Ganesh Sadashiv Patil.He Is The Student Of UG In Field Of Pharmacy.He Has Writer And Poet Who Writes 50+ Poetry In Hindi And Marathi Languages.He Loves To Write On Love,Humanity, Motivation And Social Themes.He loves to write down his feelings, his thoughts on various topics which makes him a writer of one his own kind

देश-एक सपना

मेरा एक सपना है जो मेरा अपना है साथ सबको मुझे यहा रखना है
बिखरते हुये इन रिशतो कि डोरो को मुझे बस साथ मे यहा लाना है
संग सारे जब एकसाथ हो हमारे तो हम हर मुश्किलो से लढ जाते है
सबको एकसाथ यहा करके मुझे हर घर घर में एकात्मता जो लानी है
भाईचारे से सबको सिखलाना यहा बैर ना अब मुझे अब फैलने देना है
तू मेरा और तू पराया इन बातो और पेहलियो को यहा से दूर रखना है
जात पात और धर्म की बातो से ना किसिको मुझे अब लढणे देना है
संसार सारा एक परिवार है हमारा यही बात अब सबको समजानी है
एकता से भरे हुए देश का ये सपना मेरी नजरो में यु आकर बस गया है
पुरा करुंगा ये सपना सच एक दिन मेरे देश को आगे बढाते हि जाना है

.Hetal Chaudhary

She is Hetal Ben chaudhary from Netrang in Gujarat.She is a teacher of social science.She write her write up with Nick name Krishna.She write specially microfiction,article and poem.

हमारे वीर जवान

वो अपनो से कोसो दूर होकर भी
देखो कैसे खडे है,
ठंडी, गरमी, बरसात में भी
देखो कैसे अडे है.

सरहद के चौकिदार है ये
देखो हमारी शान है ये,
गोलियों की बरसात में भी
देखो कैसे लडे हैं ये.

अपना नींद और चैन गवाके
बंदूक ताने खडे हुऐ हैं,
मा भारती की रक्षा के लिए
देखो कैसे डटे हैं ये.

दुश्मन की हरएक गोली को
अपने सीने पर झेंलेगे,
तिरंगे की शान के लिए
देखो जीद पर अडे हैं ये.

देश में चेनो -अमन रहे
बस यही उसकी अभीलाषा हैं ,
हर भाइ मेरा सलामत रहे
यही हमारी प्राथँना हैं.

सरहद का रक्षक

छोटी सी बहन जानवी कई दिनों से माता का शिर खा रही थी ,भाई कब आएगा,भाई कब आएगा। आखिर थक कर मां बोली-' रक्षाबंधन पर तेरा बड़ा भाई जरूर आएगा।'

तब से जानवी आतुरता के साथ रक्षाबंधन की राह देख रही थी।देश की सरहद का रक्षा करने वाला भाई सरहद से लौटकर आया लेकिन तिरंगे में ।।

Himanshu Ravat

Parents put his name as Himanshu Rawat. But he called himself as shayar_bychance. Yes its his insta id and passion too. Current affairs latest currently pay electricity bill of a house in Chandigarh. Like other millions of people he is also college going student who is pursuing BCom. Enthusiasm and positive minded are his qualities. A true human who loves to help people. His motto of life is to learn and explore as much as he can.

मेरा भारत सबसे प्यारा है

मेरा भारत सबसे प्यारा है
मेरा भारत सबसे प्यारा है

हिंदू के लिए मंदिर
मुसलमान के लिए मस्जिद
ईसाई के लिए गिरीजाघर
सिखों के लिए गुरुद्वारा है

मेरा भारत सबसे प्यारा है
मेरा भारत सबसे प्यारा है

आयुर्वेद,लूडो,चेस योग और
दुनिया का सबसे बड़ा अविष्कार
ज़ीरो देने वाला देश हमारा है

मेरा भारत सबसे प्यारा है
मेरा भारत सबसे प्यारा है

इंडिया,हिंदुस्तान,भारतवर्ष,आर्यावर्ता,जामबुदीप
हिन्द,नाभिवर्श
इतने ज़्यादा नामों वाला
दुनिया में अकेला देश हमारा है

मेरा भारत सबसे प्यारा है
मेरा भारत सबसे प्यारा है

दुनिया में सबसे ज्यादा धन था यहां पहले था यह सोने की चिड़िया
इतने ज्ञान ग्रंथ है यहां कि यह विश्व गुरु भी बन चुका है

और अब देखो यह अंतरिक्ष गुरु बनने जारा है

मेरा भारत सबसे प्यारा है
मेरा भारत सबसे प्यारा है

1618 भाषाओं वाला
6 ऋतुओं 6 धर्मों वाला
ऐसा देश हमारा है

मेरा भारत सबसे प्यारा है
मेरा भारत सबसे प्यारा है

Ipsita

A carefree, joyful, realistic in practical life but she enjoys to live in an imaginative and fictional world. This is Ipsita Panigrahi, a budding writer, who loves to express her feelings and emotions through writings. She hails from Bhubaneswar - the city of temples, Odisha. She has a passion for literature, as she loves to do all those stuff which makes her happy and literature is one among them. She is likely to be called as a scribbler. She finds peace in gardening and reading books and an artist is also hidden in her.

भारत के वीर सपूत....!!!

तूफ़ान से लड़ते हैं वो,
आँधियों में उड़ते हैं,
सागर में गोतें लगते हैं ,
जख्म भी भूल जाते हैं।

खून से खेलते हैं होली ,
पशीने से भी
दिए जलाते हैं ।
देश की मिट्टी में ,
अपना अंग-अंग रंगते हैं।
यूँ ही नहीं व भारत के वीर कहलाते हैं।

धरती, जल, वायु भी,
इनको नमन करते हैं,
वो भारत माँ के वीर सपूत
कहाँ किसी से डरते हैं ।

मजाल है उनका ,
जो भारत से टकराने की
कोशिश करते हैं।
शायद वे भूल जाते हैं,
भारत के वीर
आज भी जीवित हैं।

जिसने भी हात लगया ,
इस पवित्र भूमि को,
वे दुश्मन धूल चट कर गए हैं।
चाहे व कारगिल का युद्ध हो ,
या गलवान घाटी में प्रहार ,

शत्रु ने चखा है सिर्फ़ और सिर्फ़ हार ।

जवान भी बड़े महान होते हैं, महानता के
मूरत होते हैं,
नहीं आसान फौजी होना,
दूसरों की हिफाजत के लिए अपना सब
कुछ खो देना।

चलते हैं वो,आगे बढ़ते हैं,
यु हीं न थक कर
रुकते हैं ।
जान हथेली पर लेकर भी वो,
शत्रु का बिनाश करते हैं ।
वो भारत माँ के वीर सपूत,
कहाँ किसी से डरते हैं ।

वे किसी के भाई होते हैं,
तो किसी के पिता,
किसी के पति होते हैं,
तो किसी के सखा।
कभी गजरे की खुसबू को महकता छोड़ आते हैं,
कभी नन्ही सी चिड़िया को चहकता
छोड़ आते हैं,
कभी दोस्तों की टोलियों की मस्ती
छोड़ आते हैं,
तो कभी गलियों की पुकार की मिठास छोड़ आते हैं।
यु हीं नहीं वो भारत के वीर कहलाते हैं।

यूँ तो रक्षाबंधन पर अपनी बहन की
रक्षा का शपथ लेते हैं,

Jadav Manishaben

She is Jadav Manishaben Raghavbhai from Gir Gadhada Gir Somnath.She is a teacher at kulka primary school.she published her write up in online platform.and in anthology.

सपूत भारत के

आजादी के लिए जिसने ।
प्राण न्योछावर किए अपने।।
मातृभूमि की रक्षा की जिसने।
नेताजी वह सपूत भारत के।।
सुभाषचंद्र बोझ नाम था जिसका।
जानकीनाथ की संतान था वह।
देश के लिए जीवन दिया जिसने।
नेताजी वह सपूत भारत के।।
अंग्रेज जिससे देख कांपते थे।
वह भारत मां के वीर सपूत थे।।
अंग्रेज का अस्त किया भारत में।
नेताजी वह सपूत भारत के।।
अन्याय के खिलाफ जिसने आवाज उठाई थी।
देश के लिए जो मर मिटे थी
नेताजी भारत के सपूत थे।।

आजादी

राष्ट्रध्वज की सलामी से सम्मानित।
संगीत के सूर से छलक रही आजादी हमारी।।
राष्ट्रगीत के नाद से गूंज रही।
सांस्कृतिक कार्य से निखर रही आजादी। ।
शहीदों की याद से हुई ताज़ा।
देशभक्ति के रंगों में रंगी हुई आजादी।।
फूलो की सुगंध से सदा महकने वाली।
गांधीजी की यादों के साथ गुनगुना रही आजादी।।
महामुली मिल गई हमे आजादी।
रक्षा करेंगे हरवक्त आजादी की।।

Jaya Bharti Kuntal

She is Jaya bharti kuntal who is also known by the name Jaya bharti. She hails from birthplace of lord krishna MATHURA, UP, INDIA. She is a medical student, published writer, author, motivational speaker,photographer by amateur , compiler and has co-authored 35+ anthologies including 2 international anthologies. Almighty, her parents(Dharmendra Singh kuntal & pinky devi kuntal) and grandparents(Hardam singh kuntal & bhudevi kuntal)are real source of inspiration for her & she owes her success to them.Infact her father and grandfather encouraged her to go in the field of poetry.she loves playing guitar and singing.she is also a volleyball player.

देश मेरा

मेरे भारत देश की मिट्टी सोना है ।
हर दिन यहाँ का खुद में एक खूबसूरत तोहफा है ।
खेत-खलियान मेरे देश का गहना हैं ।
खेतो की हरियाली मेरे देश में हरदम लहराती है ।
हमारे अन्नदाता किसानों के कारण ही अन्न की पैदावार देश में पूर्ण तरीके से हो पाती है ।
यहाँ सब धर्मों को समान माना जाता है।
हर नागरिक को यहाँ स्वतंत्रता से बोलने का अधिकार दिया जाता है ।
हर किसी को अपनी मर्जी से जीने का अधिकार दिया जाता है।
यहाँ लोकतांत्रिक तरीके से चुनाव होते हैं अपना नेता लोग स्वइच्छा से चुनते हैं ।
यहाँ होली , दीवाली , ईद , क्रिस्मसडे ,गुरुपर्व जैसे कई त्योहार समय समय पर मनाये जाते हैं ।
ये मेरे भारत देश की "अनेकता में एकता" को दर्शाते हैं ।
यही सब खूबियाँ मेरे भारत देश को सबसे अनोखा और महान बनाती हैं ।।

Jeenal Nagotha

She is Nagotha jinalben Dinesh bhai from surat.She is student at Sanskartirth Ajol in std 12.She is clever student and write poem and article.Her wish is being manager in big company.Her wish to further study in CA

धरा बचाओ ,देश बचाओ

पानी पानी हो गया है देश मेरा पानी की इस बूंदों से
मेरे देश की नदिया भर गई है नीरो की इस बूंदों से।
आवश्यकता ने आविष्कार किया प्रकृति की इन गोदो में।
खोज परिवर्तित हुई कहानी के इस पन्नो में।
पानी पानी हो गया है देश मेरा पानी की इस बूंदों से
मेरे देश की नदिया भर गई है नीरो की इस बूंदों से।
कोई हमे बतलाता है जलवायु बदलती है ओजोन के इस छिद्रों से।
जलशीखर विकृत होते है मनुष्य के इस कृत्य से।
धूप बदलती है सूरज की इन किरणों में।
बेमोसम बारिश होती है हमारी गलियों में।
सूरज उदय हो सिरजता है प्रकृति की गलियो में।
सूरज की विवशता देखो परावैगनी किरणों में।
सायंस मैथ्स भूल जाओगे भूगोल के अंधेरे में।।
अभी सुधर जाओ वरना नीर न होगा नैनो में।

स्वच्छता से सेवा

हमारे देश की शान बढ़ानी है तो सफाई रख कर भी हम देश सेवा कर सकते है।हमारे गली , महोल्ले एवम गांव ,स्कूल सब जगह को स्वच्छ रखेंगे तो हमारा स्वास्थ्य अच्छा रहेगा,स्वस्थ मनुष्य ही देश को आर्थिक, शैक्षिक एवं सामाजिक रिती से हमारे देश को उन्नत बनाने की सेवा कर सकते है।स्वच्छता से हम सब मिलकर अपने देश को उन्नत बना सकते है।

स्वच्छ रहो ,सुरक्षित रहो
देश की सेवा करो ।।

Jeevitha S.

Here is Miss.Jeevitha Sundararajan, who is a budding compiler and author . She has published her writeups as a Co-author in 100+ books. She is a girl with stupendous writing skills. Her heart is a castle abound with unbreakable courage, being contained with enticing dreams. Penning is her way of spreading aesthetic vibes among her readers. Being a literarian is her pride. She can't stop being awesome because it's in her blood. She loves to be a unicorn amidst the flock of sheeps ! She is the one who would give all of her to make her parents proud.

Instagram @miss.sundar_writes

My Beloved Nation !

The country which inspired others through its custom and traditional values!
When others admired about development and facilitates about foreigners,
Foreigners admired our country's rituals.
We have been wise in all aspects of tradition ,
Growing out from colonialism we stand independent now;
We are great in all aspects ,
We inspire; we stand as a good example for others.
No one would disagree with the richness of our values.
Patriotism towards our country lies in every single cell in our body !
Jai hind ! Let Hindustan be unique and spread vibrance everywhere…

Jyotsna Raval

She is Raval jyotsana Ben from Netrang.She is the head teacher in the school.She write online mode.She write five hundred up write up at online.

એક સૈનિકની પત્ની

હસીને સહેલી વેદના ગૌરવ બને છે ત્યારે સ્ત્રી ની વેદનાના મૂંગા આક્રંદ ગૌરવના એ આભાસી સંતોષમાં દબાઈ જાય છે .એક સ્ત્રી સૈનિક ની પત્ની હોય કે સામાન્ય સ્ત્રી પણ પોતાના પતિની જુદાઈની વેદના અનુભવે જ સમજાય છે. એક સ્ત્રી જ સ્ત્રીની વેદના સમજી શકે છે .

સંધ્યાના જીવનમાં પણ આવેલી વેદનાઓના ઘટમાળ ચોરીના ચાર ફેરા ફર્યા પછી અનુભવાયા. સુરજ એક ભારતીય સીમા રક્ષક દળમાં કાશ્મીરની સરહદ પર બર્ફીલા પહાડો પર સૈનિકની ભૂમિકા ભજવતો હતો. ગુજરાતના નાનકડા પહાડી વિસ્તારોમાં હરિયાળા ડુંગરોની છાયામાં ઉછેર પામેલ સૂરજની લશ્કરી દળમાં ભરતી થતા એની કઠોર ટ્રેનિંગ પૂરી થતા કાશ્મીરની સરહદ પર પોસ્ટીંગ થયું .કાશ્મીરની સરહદ પર રાત દિવસ બર્ફીલા પહાડો પર માતાની સેવા કરવા સુરજ તત્પર હતો .સંધ્યાની સાથે વિતેલી ક્ષણો યાદ કરતો હતો. સંધ્યા પણ સુરજ સાથે સમય પસાર કરવાના સપનામાં ખોવાઈ જતી.આવનારી એકલતા અને પતિના વિયોગથી બેખબર .

સંધ્યા અને સુરજના લગ્ન નક્કી થઈ ગયા .સરહદ પરથી લાંબી રજા લઈ સુરજ લગ્ન માટે આવ્યો. સંધ્યા અને સુરજ ચોરીના ચાર ફેરા ફરી સાત જનમના વચન નિભાવવા ની કસમ ખાઈને જીવનની શરૂઆત કરી. બંને સુંદર જીવનની કલ્પના કરતા દમણના દરિયા કિનારે ફરવા ગયા .દરિયાના વિશાળ મોજા નો અવાજ સાંભળીને બંને યુગલ કલાકો સુધી વાતો કરતા. સુરજ

સંધ્યાને પોતાની ફરજ વિશે સમજાવતો ,દિવસો સુધી ઘરે નહિ અવાય તો ચિંતા નહીં કરતી, શાંતિથી મમ્મી-પપ્પા સાથે રહેજે, હું સમયે આવી જઈશ અને હંમેશા ખુશ રહેજે. મૂક સંમતિ આપી સંધ્યા ફક્ત માથું હલાવ્યું .

એક મહિનો વીતી ગયો સૂરજ અને સંધ્યા સાથે વિદાય લેવાની વેળા આવી .વસમી વિદાય આપતા સંધ્યાની આંખમાં આંસુ આવી અટકી ગયા. સૂરજને આપેલું વચન યાદ આવતા સંધ્યા રડી પણ ન શકી . સંધ્યા એકલી-અટૂલી રૂમમાં પતિના વિયોગની વેદના સહેતા રહેતી. સુરજ ને સમય મળતા વિડીયો કોલ કરતો નેટ આવે એવી જગ્યાએ પોતાની પત્નીને સમજાવતો સંધ્યાને સુરજ ની કમી મહેસૂસ થતી હતી એટલે વિડીયો કોલ આવે ત્યારે અધીરી બની સુરજ સાથે ઘણો સમય વાતો કરતી .

તેનાંથી દૂર રહીને જીવવાથી સંધ્યા અસંતોષ ની લાગણી અનુભવવા લાગી.સુરજને દિવસો સુધી બર્ફીલા પહાડો પર રહેવાનું થવાથી સંધ્યા સાથે વાત નહોતો કરી શકતો .સંધ્યાને સતત ચિંતા હતી. આંતકવાદી હુમલા ટીવી પર જોયા એટલે રાત દિવસ સુરજ માથે સંકટ નો આવે એવી પ્રાર્થના કરતી. ફફડતે હૈયે જીવતી .એને દૂર રહેતા પતિના ખોરાક કપડાં થી માંડી નાની-નાની બાબતોની ચિંતા થતી .સંધ્યા સુરજ ના ફોટા મોબાઇલમાં જોતી ક્યારેક સુરજ સાથે વિતાવેલી ક્ષણો યાદ કરતી. આમ તરફડતી તરફડતી દિવસો કાઢતી. સમય મળતા સુરજ વિડીયો કોલ કરતો ત્યારે કસમ તોડી એ ચોધાર આંસુ

Kajal Sah

मेरा नाम काजल साह है, मैं दसवीं की छात्रा हुँ, मुझे अपने विचार सभी के सामने प्रस्तुत करना बेहद पसंद है, और मैंने यह विचार अपने कविता, कहानियाँ, निबंध के माध्यम से प्रस्तुत की, मेरी पहली कविता मैंने लड़कियों के विषय पर लिखा था, और उस कविता का शीर्षक था :मुझे जीने दो, यह कविता मेरी सोशल मीडिया के लोंगो को बेहद पसंद आई, जब उनका प्यार मिलने लगा तब मेरे लिखने की कला और बड़ी तेज़ी से बढ़ने लगी, तब से मैंने अपनी कविताओं को लगाम नहीं दिया और हर विषय को नया बनाने की लत लग गई, और साहित्य को मैंने अपने जीवन का एक अनमोल हिस्सा माना मेरी प्रिय लेखिका महादेवी वर्मा जी है और मुझे उनकी रचनाएँ बेहद पसंद और आशा से भरपूर लगता है, जिस प्रकार उन्होंने जीवन के हर संघर्ष को हिम्मत से पार किया ठीक उसी प्रकार मैं भी अपने जीवन के हर संघर्ष

से हिम्मत से लँड़ूगी और दिखा दूंगी नारी कमजोर नहीं, महाशक्ति की पहचान है.

मेरा प्यार देश

मुझे अपने भारत से प्यार है
क्युकी भारत मेरा अभिमान है
ना जाति का करता कोई भेद
ना धर्म में कोई मतभेद
सारे धर्मो को हमेशा अपनाता
इसलिए भारत मेरा सबसे श्रेष्ठ कहलाता।

समय कठिन था
लेकिन भारत ने हमें हंसकर लड़ना सिखाया
हर हालातों से हमें डटकर चलना सिखाया
हमें आत्मनिर्भर का सही अर्थ
समझाया
तीन अक्षर एकता शब्द में
हमें बंधना सिखाया
हमारा अभिमान और बढ़ाया
मेरे मनोबल को और साहस दिलाया
मुझे अपने भारत से प्यार है
क्युकी भारत मेरा अभिमान है।

बच्चों का प्यारा भारत

हम नए भारत के बच्चे है
नहीं किसी से हम डरते है
सारे मुसीबत को हिम्मत से पार करते है
हम नए दौर के बच्चे है
जो मुश्किल है
उसे हंस कर आसान बनाते है
जो जुल्म करते है
उन्हें सजा दिलाते है
हम नए भारत के वीर बच्चे है।
छल कपट से जिसने किया
हम भारतीयों पर शासन
अब नहीं सहेंगे
किसी गोरे का शासन
मिटाएंगे वो सारे बुरे कुरीतियों को
और नहीं बनाएंगे किसी भारतीयों
को किसी गोरे का गुलाम
अब भारत नहीं रहा १९ वीं सदी जैसा
बन चुका है ,भारत वीरों की कुर्बानियों से
महलों जैसा
हम नए भारत के बच्चे है
और अपने कर्तव्य से कभी नहीं हटते है
भारत को अपने मेहनत से महान बनाते है।
धन्यवाद🙏 काजल साह -

Kareena Verma

she is is a computer science student it and co author of many anthologies and just like her name Kareena delineate alike her name , sanguine with her soul, pure with her heart , innocent with her straightforward thoughtful perceptions!
For her Rectitude within her is everything & nothing is above than Viracity with our nation , she wants only to flame alike terracotta Diya, for one day she'll spread the happiness of lights as the most bright star in the sky of someone home and wanna to spread love of humanity every where!

आर्यवर्त

मैं हिन्दू हूं , मैं मुस्लिम हूं ।
मैं सीख , ईसाई के घरों के
परिवारो में जन जन की
पली बढ़ी की संतान हूं
मैं मंदिर में जलती ज्योति हूं
मैं मस्जिद में चढ़ाई जाने वाली चादर हुं ,
मै चर्चो में रोशनी फैलाने वाली मोमबत्ती हूं
मैं वो इंसान हूं जो
इंसानियत का पाठ पढ़ाती है
जो मजहबों में भेदभाव ना
रखने में विश्वास ना रखती है ।
मैं इंसान हूं और
इंसानियत का धर्म में ही विश्वास रखतीं हूं
मैं इंसानियत के मजहब का पाठ पढ़ाती हुं
मैं वासुदेव कुटुंबकम् के देश में
जन्मी भारत देश की निवासी हूं ।

My Oath

Throughout The from my Birth ,
I have solely every Tenets of my life ,
The fulsome Volition and Verdicts towards my aim.
Always be rife of full of VERACITY regime in Bottom of my heart.

I indoctrinated to my destiny nither Be allow to Loathe to someone ever.
That's how much they gave me painful life.but while is always incresing my ENDURANCE.

My soul has disparated from the crowd,I keen to straved, Disquieting for youIN
If I shall quietus for my country,so only in my Motherland Outskirts.
I wanna be again Resuscitate to myself.
Do and Die for my countrymen,for my Motherland

Kavita Modi

She is member of CDRDC, president of giants Group of Reva,writer,translater, organizer, Anchor, co-ordinator.

देश के युवा सब आओ
विवेकानंद सा बने महान
नाम अमर कर देशका
बढ़ाते हमारे देश की शान
मर्यादित शिक्षित हम बने सदा
करें देश का सम्मान सदा
जहां कहीं भी जाते विश्व में
भारत का मान बढाये विश्व में।
वेद धर्म को अपने पहले जानो
नित्य तुम ज्ञान अच्छे सुनो
देश के लिए समय पर मरना जानो
समय आने पर हो कुर्बान।
देश के युवा सब आओ
विवेकानंद सा बने महान।

रचयिता-कविता मोदी
भरूच-गुजरात

भारत माता
आओ मेरे वीर जवानों
भारत माता तुम्हें पुकारती।
गद्दारों को सबक सिखादो
भारत माता तुम्हें पुकारती।
जाति-धर्म से उपर-उठकर
निज कर्तवय र्निभाना है।
कहती है मां भारती
राष्ट्र धर्म है सबसे उपर
बाकी सब कहने का ताना-बाना है।

हिन्दुस्तान में रहने वाला
पक्का न हिन्दुस्तानी है
इसकी ओर जो आंख उठाते
उसकी नजरें झुकानी है।
यही कमाते यही का खाते
और गद्दारों से हाथ मिलाते
ऐसों को तुम सबक सिखा दो
कहती है मां भारती।
हर नारी की रक्षा करना
पहला कर्तव्य तुम्हारा है
राखी की महिमा को निभाओ।
उसका एक ही नारा है।
देशके दुश्मन ऐसे हैं।
जो दंगे करवाते हैं।
अपने मतलब की खातिर
जनता को लगवाते हैं।
राम-कृष्ण की धरती है यह।
गौतम बुद्ध की माता है।
सत्य अहिंसा के साथ हमें भी

सबक सिखाना है।
ऐसों को तुम सबक सिखा दो।
कहती है माता भजागो मेरे जवानों
भारत माता तुम्हें पुकारती।

Krishna Motvani

Krishna Motwani is a Student currently.
She use to pen down her feelings.
She is a moody girl.
She started writing in the month of june,2020.
She writes in her free time.
She writes some motivational quotes or poetries too and practices artworks also.
She lives her life like a bird
As bird flies freely and enjoys life like that she also lives her life freely and enjoy fullest.
For motivating and inspiring poems and quotes,

भारत है हमारी शान,
यहाँ हर एक का किया जाता है सम्मान।

रहते है सब एकता से,
और सम्मानता से।

सब त्यौहार मनाए जाते है साथ,
हर मुश्किल में देते है एक दूसरे का साथ।

कुछ है एसी चीज़े जो नहीं होनी चाहिए,
बस यही आशा है वो सब भी जल्द ही बदलना चाहिए।

लड़की को बहार नहीं निकाला जाता,
लड़का लड़की में फर्क है होता।

एक उम्मीद है सब ठीक हो जाएगा,
अपना भारत फिर जगमगाएगा।

माँ का स्वरूप भारत है,

Miral Purohit

She is Miral purohit from Rajula.She is a collage student at dvp collage devaka.She write drama ,poem and article.She won many prize in essay compition.

हिन्दुस्तानी"

सरज़मी ये हमारी, गुरुर हमारा है,
ना हिन्द हारेगा कभी, ना कभी हारा है।

देख ले तू पलटाके, पन्ने इतिहास के,
सजाया है हमने इनको, स्वर्ण के अल्फ़ाज़ से।

चाहे बापू, चाहे चाचा, देख लो सरदार को,
हो वो तात्या या बिस्मिल, आज़ाद असरदार हो।

खिलाया गुलिस्ता उन्होंने, अपने बलिदान से,
उन्हींकी बदौलत, हम जीते है स्वाभिमान से।

छलकता है सबमे यहां, प्रेम रंग श्वेत सा,
रखते है ये दिलमे जज़्बा, मरुस्थल की रेत सा।

खड़ा है जो सरहद पे वो, शान-ए-हिन्दुस्तान है,
हर जवान हमारा गर्व, हमारा अभिमान है।

छोड़ आया वो पीछे खुशियां, उन महकती राहो में,
तरसता है मां का आंचल, लेने उसको बाहो में।

खाना, पीना, हंस के जीना, रखते हम ईमान है,
हर घड़ी में साथ हमारे, खड़ा हर किसान है।

उत्तर में अडिखम हिम जेसे, हमारा रखवैया है,
बहके वहां से पावन करती, हमको गंगा मैया है।

ना वो हिन्दु, ना वो मुस्लिम, हम सब एक इंसान है,

साथ मे पढ़ते हम गीता, पढ़ते कुरान है।

करेंगे हम हिफाज़त, ये मुल्क हमारी जान है,
हंसते हंसते ये जिंदगी, इसपे कुर्बान है।

आन देश की, शान देश की, हम देश के संतान है,
हम है हिन्दुस्तानी, हमारी यही पहचान है।

Mohanpriya K

Co-author Mohanapriya.K is a good writer from Tamilnadu, India. She has completed her Bachelor's degree in Engineering stream. She has been a writer for one year as her passion. She wants to be a best compiler and curator in future. Yet she sincerely hope that this writing journey of her will bring her many successes. She also loves singing.

My Country – India

My homeland is India.
I like my country very much.
The country where we were born is as precious as our mother.
How many resources of my country!
How many specials of my country!
India is a democracy.
It is the only country where people of all languages live together despite the fact that they speak many languages.
The national bird of India is the peacock.
The tiger is the national animal of India.
There are many tourist sites in my country so much fun to look around.
People from many cultures and beliefs live here.
But everyone's only hope is that everyone can live together even if they follow different cultures.

I Love My India – Jai Hind

India is a country of patriotic youth who will do anything for their country.
I am very proud to be Indian.
A country with talented women who make many achievements.
Not only then but also today is a proud country where everyone volunteers for the country.
Because we all know very well what the importance of achieving freedom is.
So we never fail to give our housewives the freedom they deserve.
Women are all deities of our country.
That is why we call the rivers of our country by women's names, which help to produce crops and supply water.
Jai Hind!

Mohanpriya S.K.

Mohana priy.S.K, a literature student has written many poems, quotes and short story under the pen name called"MONA". She started writing her works at the age of 19. All of her works are simple, humorous, understandable and raising questions.

Mere Dil India.

India a mesmerizing country !
Which was loved by everyone,
It is the country which faced lots and lots of struggles for independence,
Though it is not the devoleped as a country, but it was developed as a good hearted person !
India was so lovable with lots of cultures, festivals, languages !
Many countries may celebrate their festivals in grand way,
But in india, each and every day will be celebrated in grand manner,
How much ever problem arises, india
Will join hands together and rebuild together with happyest face !
Even you may live in different countries, but not all country will be as same as "INDIA".

Namrata Oza

She is Namrata oza from Ahemdabad.She write her write up with Nick name Surbhi.She is a housewife.She was teach as hindi proffesior 1 year.She write in
Save Banass news and jung a gujrat news paper.She write many type of literature like story,micro tale,song,haiku etc.

સાચી આઝાદી

જો પ્રજાને મળતો હોય યોગ્ય ન્યાય,
તો તે દેશ પ્રજાસત્તાક કહી શકાય

વીર જવાનો સરહદ પર શહીદી વહોરે,
ભ્રષ્ટ નેતાઓ પોતાની તિજોરી ધનથી ભરે

પ્રજાનું અવિરત શોષણ થાય,
ક્યારેક મોંઘવારી ,ક્યારેક કર વસુલાત કરાય

અસામાજિક તત્વોને સન્માન અપાય,
આદર્શવાદીઓની વિવશતાનો ફાયદો ઉઠાવી અપમાનિત
કરાય

કોઈ નીડર બની અન્યાયનો કરે વિરોધ,
તેની પ્રગતિ અને સક્ષમતાને તોડી સૌ કરે તેમાં અવરોધ

નારીનું ના થતું સન્માન કે ના મળતી સ્વતંત્રતા,
હરપળ નિયમો અને રિવાજોના નામે મળતી પરતંત્રતા

ઘણી જહેમત ઉઠાવી બંધારણ ઘડયા,
છતાં ક્યાં દેશમાં તે પ્રમાણે હક અને ફરજો મળ્યા?

જે દેશમાં મહાન વ્યક્તિઓ એ અવતાર ધર્યો,
તે દેશમાં સંસ્કાર અને સંસ્કૃતિનો વિધ્વંશ થઈ રહ્યો.

Nilofar Farooqui Tauseef

Meet our co-author Nilofar Farooqui Tauseef, born and brought up from Bihar Sharif, Nalanda but living in Mumbai. She is Software Engineer in IT and loves penning down her thoughts, emotions through her writing. For her “Pen is a sword to bring revolution”. She wants to make a new changes in life by the motivational quotes or speeches. You can check her fb and instagram handled

भारत मेरी शान

भारत माता का, स्वाभिमान नही खोने देंगे।
भारत मेरी शान है, अभिमान नही खोने देंगे।

हो जाएंगे कुर्बान, अपने देश की खातिर,
किया जो वचन तुझसे, नीलाम नही होने देंगे।

लहू से लिख जाएँगे, वतन पे नाम अपना,
रक्षा हेतु, बेकसूरों का बलिदान नही होने देंगे।

खींच गयी जी दीवारें, मज़हब के नाम पे,
अब कोई जात-पात का निशान नहीं होने देंगे।

सभ्यता संस्कृति ही है, सौंदर्य आर्यवर्त का
किसी गद्दारों की खातिर, बदनाम नहीं होने देंगे।

तिरंगा बन जायेगा, चार लहू मेरे रंग से,
झुक कर कभी भारत का, अपमान नहीं होने देंगे।
झुक कर कभी भारत का, अपमान नहीं होने देंगे।

तुझपे जान लुटाऊँ माँ

धरती पीली, अम्बर नीला,
तुझको शीष झुकाऊं माँ।
तेरी ही माटी का मैं गुड्डा,
तुझपे जान लुटाऊं माँ।

जन्म दिया जिस माँ ने,
उसका भी कर्तव्य निभाऊं माँ।
आँख करे जो तिरछी तुझपे,
उसको चीर के आऊँ माँ।

तेरी आन की खातिर मैं,
शहीद भी हो जाऊं माँ।
लिपट कर आऊँ तिरंगा में,
तेरी मिट्टी से लिपट जाऊँ माँ।

गद्दारों को निकाल देश से,
चुनर तेरी धानी कर जाऊँ माँ।
आन , बान, शान है तू मेरी
कैसे तुझे भुलाऊं माँ।

पापी का नाश कर मैं
तेरी गंगा में नहाऊं माँ
बांध चलूं मैं कफ़न सर पे
दुश्मन से टकरा जाऊँ माँ

नमन करूँ शीष झुकाऊं
जान अर्पित कर जाऊँ माँ
तेरी ही माटी का मैं गुड्डा,
तुझपे जान लुटाऊं माँ।

Parul Amit

She is Parulben Amitbhai.She publish her write up with Nick name Pankhudi.She is branch manager in SBI.She published eight book and many co book.Her many stories,poem and article published in news paper like Nibhav Dainik,Gandhinagar Metro,Hitkalin news paper.She write specially love.Her five hundred up write up are based on love theme.She is also daily coulamist in news paper and group admin of Angat Dairy.

આંધળા પશ્ચિમી કરણને ડામી
 સ્વદેશી વસ્તુને પ્રાધાન્ય આપીએ'.

સ્વદેશી ચળવળ એ ભારતીય સ્વતંત્રતા વખતે એક મહત્વનો ભાગ હતી, આજે પણ મહત્વ નો ભાગ બની ગઈ છે, ભારતીય અર્થતંત્ર ને ડગમગતુ અટકાવવા માટે.
ભારતીયોએ અપનાવાયેલી આ એક આર્થિક નિતી હતી જેનો ઉદ્દેશ્ય ગુલામીને હટાવવાની સાથે અંગ્રેજ સરકારની સત્તાને હલાવવાનો હતો.
અને અત્યારે એનું મહત્વ એટલું જ આંકી શકાય,ગુલામી એક મહાવિનાશક રોગ કોરોનાની.
ચાલો આત્મ નિર્ભર કરીએ આપણા ભારત દેશને ભારતીય ઉધ્યોગોને સદ્ધર અને દેશને સ્વાવલંબી બનાવીએ.
વિદેશી પ્રોડક્ટસનો બહિષ્કર માત્ર મેસેજ ફોરવર્ડ કરી ને નહીં, પણ સ્વદેશી માલ-વસ્તુનું ખરીદી- વેચાણ કરીએ.
આપણે જાતે વિચારી નથી શકતા કે આત્મનિર્ભર માટે શું કરવું.
પણ જયારે દેશના વડાપ્રધાન આપણને ભારતમાં બનેલી વસ્તુઓનો ઉપયોગ કરવાની એક અપીલ કરી હતી જે આપણે ભૂલી ગયા છીએ.
તો શું એને આપણે અનુસરીના શકીએ?
જો સ્વદેશીને આપણે મક્કમ પણે નિયમ બનાવી અપનાવી લઈએ તો ચોક્કસ આવનારા સમયમાં ભારતને વિશ્વના નેતૃત્વ કરવાનો માર્ગ મળી જશે.
ને આમાં અઘરું શું છે?
આપણા માટે, સ્વ માટે સ્વદેશી અપનાવવું એ એક ગૌરવ ભર્યું હોવું જોઈએ.

માનવ જીવનમાં આટલા મોટા પરિવર્તન આવ્યા બાદ ચાલો થોડું પરિવર્તન તરફ પ્રયાણ કરી લઈએ.

સવારના બ્રશ થી લઇ, ચા,કોફી નાસ્તો, કપડાં, લંચ,ડિનરમાં નજીવા ફેરફાર લાવી દઈએ.

મનમાં ચાલી રહેલા કેટ કેટલાયે આંદોલનને પહોંચી વાળવા ચાલો સ્વદેશી આંદોલન ઊભું કરી દેશને આર્થિક રૂપથી મજબૂત કરવા મંડી પડીએ.

કોવિડ 19 ને કારણે સમગ્ર દુનિયાની અર્થવ્યવસ્થા હાલક ડોલક થઈ ગઈ છે ત્યારે દેશને આત્મનિર્ભર બનાવવા માટે વધારેમાં વધારે સ્વદેશી લોકલ પ્રોડક્ટસનો ઉપયોગ કરીએ.

નવનિર્માણથી જ મૂલ્ય અંકાય છે,

કરી લઈએ મનમાં જ એક આંદોલન સ્વદેશી ને મક્કમ પણે અપનાવવાનું વલણ. આર્થિક અસલામતીનો પડઘો ત્યાં જ સમી જશે.

મરજી દેશની છે એની પકડ અકબંધ રહે તેનું ધ્યાન રાખવું જ પડશે.

તો જ નિશ્ચિત પરિમાણ આવશે.

તો ચાલો સ્વદેશી વસ્તુને પ્રાધાન્ય આપીએ.

"ચાલો પાછો આવ્યો એક ગાંધી
સ્વદેશીની હવે બુમરાણ ચાલી
યુગોથી અણસમજુ રહ્યો માનવી
વિદેશીની ઘેલછા જોરદાર ચાલી
પણ, છે ચિત્ર આજે આશા ભર્યું
રેંટિયો આવી ગયો ને હર ગલી જાગી
કરી દઈએ પુરી ભારતની આર્થિક તંગી
કરવાનું શું માત્ર !બસ વ્યવહાર સ્વદેશી"

Parmar Rutu

She is Parmar RutuBen Rameshbhai from Ahemdabad.She study 9th at Sanskaartirth Ajol.She write many type of literature like Poem,article and story.

જાગો યુવાનો જાગો

જાગો જાગો ભારતના નવયુવાનો જાગો
દેશ દુનિયાએ જાણી ,હિંદ ભૂમિ તણી કહાની.
જાગો જાગો ભારતના નવયુવાનો જાગો
શિવાજી ખપી ગયા દેશ કાજ
લક્ષ્મીજી એ આપી મર્દાનગી ની વાટ
જાગો જાગો ભારતના નવયુવાનો જાગો
જેની છાપ ઇતિહાસ મા સુવર્ણ અક્ષરે લખાઇ
રાજગુરુ સુખદેવ ભગતસિંહે આપી દેશને વિદાઈ
જાગો જાગો ભારતના નવયુવાનો જાગો
ગાંધી બોલ્યા કાગ શ્વાન ના મોતે મરીશ
આઝાદ હિંદ સ્વરાજ લઈને પાછો ફરીશ
જાગો જાગો ભારતના નવયુવાનો જાગો
તમે આમ ન ગુમાવો નૂર
આંધળા અનુકરણ નો લઈ સૂર
જાગો જાગો ભારતના નવયુવાનો જાગો
ઉપવાસ વિરોધ સ્વીકૃતિ જેવા પાઠ સમજાયા
નેતા વિરો આઝાદ દેશ કાજ મરી મીટાયા...
જાગો જાગો ભારતના નવયુવાનો જાગો
ગાંધી આવ્યા લાકડી ટેકે
સત્ય અહિંસાની ઢાલે
જાગો જાગો ભારતના નવયુવાનો જાગો

કેસરિયા ઓઢ્યા માથા કપાયા
ત્યારે દેખાયો આઝાદ હિંદ નો સૂરજ
જાગો જાગો ભારતના નવયુવાનો જાગો

Pinky Maheta

नाम :पिंकी महेता शाह "दिशा"
शहर: अमदावाद. गुजरात.
स्टोरी मिरर मे 2018 मे Best
Other nominet.
2018 में स्टोरी मिरर मे ज्यूरी.
बैस्ट कवियित्री अवार्ड स्टोरी
मिरर से मिला हे.
बैस्ट महिला पोएट अवार्ड स्टोरी मिररकी और से.
लीटरलीकर्नल अवार्ड स्टोरी मिरर की और से.
15-11-2019को मे vajr world
रेकोर्ड मिला है!

"मेरा देश मेरा गुरुर."

अपने आपको दीया हमने वचन
जब तक होगी सांस तनमें
तब तक होंगे कुरबान हम
नाम वतनके.

वतनके नाम अपना सबकुछ
कर देंगे
जरुरत होने पर जानकी बाजी
लगा देंगे
देशके लिए कतरा कतरा खून बहा देंगे.

जन्मभूमिकी रक्षाके लिए शहादत मंजूर हे
सरहद पे तैनातमें खडे सैनिकों पर हमे नाझ हे
ये वो देश हे जिसके कण कण में लोगोकी आस्था बसी हे

यहा जहा पत्थरों में भी भगवान बसते हे
यहा सरिता,वृक्षो और अग्निको लोग देव मानते हे
यहा लोग कहे गये वचन के लिए जिंदगीभर निभाते हे.

यहा पर लोग धर्मके नाम अपनी संपत्ति दानमें देते हे
यहा पर कई धर्मके लोग
मिल जुलकर साथ रहेते हे
यहा पर लोग एक दूसरेके गम
भी तो बांटना जानते हे .

यहा पर विभिन्न तरीके ज
परस्पर एकदूसरेको अपनाकर
प्यार से जीते .है

Pravin Patel

He is Patel Pravinbhai Dayalaji bhai.He write with his Nick name Kantasut.He is a higher secondary teacher at Ambavadi Ahemdabad.He write on the spot poem,article and drama.

देशभक्ति

मेरा परम सौभाग्य मानता हूँ कि आज मुझे एक ऐसे अनोखे विषय पर अपनी कलम और दिल चलाने का अवसर मिला!जो।दुनिया का सबसे सुंदर शब्द है,जो है देश। देश शब्द की परिभाषा अपने आप मे अनोखी है।मेरे हिसाब से जँहा अर्थात कोई निश्वीत भूभाग को देश का नाम दिया जाता है। जिसमे कई वर्षों से कोई प्रजा रहती हो।
जिनकीसंस्कृति,भाषा,आचार,विचार,धर्म, पोशाक, परंपरा........ लगभग एक जैसी हो।

पर मैं जिस देश मे जन्मा हूँ, वह दुनिया का सबसे अनूठा,अलबेला,रंगीला एक मात्र देश है!और मैं मुझे अपनी जात को गर्वान्वित मानता हूँ कि मेरा जन्म इस देश में हुआ है! जिनका नाम भारत !! हा सही सुना भारत है!!नाम ही काफी है, कितना सुन्दर मन मनभावन नाम है! भारत!!!

अब मुख्य बात की तरफ आगे बढ़ते है, देश शब्द से एक शब्द आदि अनादि काल से जुड़ा हुआ है और वो है देशभक्ति!!! देशभक्ति देश से जुड़ी है और देशभक्त से जुड़ी है।

भक्ति वो ही कर सकता है जो सर्व प्रथम मन वचन कर्म से सच्चा भक्त हो,औऱ भक्त तब बन सकता है,जब उसके दिलमे ईश्वर के प्रति अनुराग हो,श्रद्धा हो!! और श्रद्धा तब पनपती जब कोई मानव में या कंही भी ऐश्वर्य शक्ति का अहेसास हो,या किसी व्यक्ति या कोई स्थल का हम पर प्रभाव हो या जो हमारी सुखाकारी जिनसे हो।

आज हम वही बात फिर से दोहराते है अलग अंदाज ,अलग रूप में अलग ढंग से। जिस तरह माँ हमारा लालन पालन करती है तो हम सब उनकी पूजा करते है कि नही?उनकी सेवा करते है कि नहीं? क्यो? क्योंकि हमने जब पहली बार आँख खोली तो प्रथम किसको देखा माँ को,

हमने प्रथम अमृत अपने मुख में किसके द्वारा पिया? माँ के द्वारा? हमने प्रथम निवाला किसके हाथ का खाया? बेशक !माँ के हाथ से!हमने पहली बार जो शब्द बोला तो क्या बोला ? माँ!..हम पहली बार किसकी उँगली पकड़कर जिंदगी का पहला कदम धरती माँ पर रखा? तो माँ का!!!! सिर्फ माँ का...मतलब की हमारी जिंदगी संवारने में जिसका सर्वाधिक योगदान रहा तो माँ का... है....।तो हम माँ की सेवा करते है ने? माँ ही हमारी खुदा और माँ के बंदे अर्थात भक्त!!

यह तो हमारी जन्मदात्री माँ के योगदान की बात हुई!। पर आज हम, और हमारी संस्कृति ने जिन्हें माँ का दरज्जा दिल से दिया है वह माँ है हमारा मादरे वतन! शिष्ट भाषा मे बोले तो मातृभूमि अर्थात देश!!।हमारा देश भारत और हम उनकी सब संतान! जिस तरह माँ का किरदार हमारे जीवन मे है,बस उसी तरह का किरदार मातृभूमि हमारे लिए निभाती है,देश निभाता है। जो माँ जिनके आँचल में रखकर सदा हम सबको बेपनाह महोबत करती है, निस्वार्थ अपना सबकुछ हम पर न्योछावर करती है!!
वो है हमारी मातृभूमि!
जीवन की मुख्य तीन आवश्यकता में जो आता है रोटी,कपड़ा और मकान!। ये कौन हमे देता है? देश अर्थात हमारे देश की मिट्टी!! वो मिट्टी नही है,वो भी हमरी माँ है,माँ जिस तरह हमारा लालन पालन करती है उसी तरह हमारी मातृभूमि भी हमारा लालन पालन करती है। हम जो खुली हवा में जो साँस ले ते है वो भी उन्हीं की देन हैं। आज हमने जो भी प्रगति की है
वो सब उन्ही की बदौलत है,उन्ही के आशीर्वाद का फल है!! जो आज हम सब बड़े चाव से खा रहे है!!!

अंत मे गागर में सागर की तरह मैं अपना विचार बोले तो विचार आपके सन्मुख रखता हूँ । जिस तरह हम अपनी माँ की भक्ति करते है,उसी तरह हमें हमे मातृभूमि की भी अपने वाणी,वर्तन,वयवहार,आचरण से शुद्ध भाव से सेवा यानी कि भक्ति करनी चाहिये!

Pritti Bhat

वह प्रिती बहन जिग्नेशभाई भट्ट है।वह नवसारी गुजरात से एक शिक्षिका है।वाचन,लेखन,संगीत सुनना एवम् अभिनय करना उनका शोख है।वह गद्य और पद्य दोनों में लिखती है। स्क्रिप्ट राइटर भी है।उनको कई सारे पुरस्कार मिले है।जैसे की लय प्रलय संस्था की और से एवम् नेक्षस सूरत से श्रेष्ठ कहानी के लिए,साहित्य क्षेत्र में विशिष्ट व्यक्ति का सम्मान नवसारी नगरपालिका द्वारा।

स्वतंत्रता दिन

तिरंगा पर लहेरा हुआ आज आजादी का पर्व।
आया आया स्वातंत्र्य दिन का पर्व।।
मन मेरा थनगनाट करे थोड़ा सा झुरता।
मन मेरा पूर्व के काले करतूत से डरता।।
युवा के खून से केसरिया गर्व ।
आया आया स्वातंत्र्य दिन का पर्व।।

गांधीजी,भगतसिंह कितने विरोने दी बलिदानी।
जिसको आरक्षण की रक जक से पड़ेगी गवानी।।
उठो युवा और लो सारे साथ में संकल्प और करो संघर्ष।
आया आया स्वातंत्र्य दिन का पर्व।।
जातिवाद कहा तक टीकेंगा आ◌े हिंदुस्तान।
सुभाष नहीं आएगा आएगा तकवादी शैतान।।
सुनहरे किरण से एकता का आए निष्कर्ष।
आया आया स्वातंत्र्य दिन का पर्व।।

तिरंगा पर लहेरा हुआ आज आजादी का पर्व।
आया आया स्वातंत्र्य दिन का पर्व।।

Rashmi Baweja

रश्मी इस कहानी की लेखिका बिल्कुल अपने नाम के अनुरूप ही सबके जीवन को प्रकाशित करती है। रश्मी हरियाणा के सोनीपत जिले की निवासी है। उन्होंने MCA किया है। उन्होंने अपना लेखन कार्य 2016 में प्रारंभ किया। वे बहुत ही स्पष्ट वादी है।वे फेसबुक पर HEART TOUCHING पेज पर भी लिखती हैं।https://www.facebook.com/rashmibaweja1993/अलग अलग विषयों पर वे बहुत अच्छा लिखती हैं। उनकी रचनाएँ पढ़कर दिल को सुकून मिलता है। दूसरों के मनोभावों को वे बखूबी समझती हैं। अपने अनुभवों व दूसरों को समझने के अपने हुनर के आधार पर ही वे अपनी रचना लेकर आई हैं। उन्हें इसके लिए बहुत बधाई!
मेरा भारत महान

दुनिया के किसी भी देश मे चले जाओ।
तुम आसमान की ऊंचाइयों तक पहुँच जाओ।
पर मेरे भारत की तो बात ही निराली है।
इससे दूर रहकर तो हर खुशी बेगानी है।

मेरे भारत मे तो दुश्मनो को भी दोस्त बनाते है।
खुशी खुशी ये अपनो पर जान भी वार देते है।
कोई कितना भी गलत करे हमारे साथ।
ये भारतीय ही है जो नफरत को प्यार में बदल डालते है।

यँहा की संस्कृति को देखकर हर कोई चकित रहता है।
यँहा जैसे रिश्तो में अपनापन और प्यार कंही नज़र नही आता है।
लोग तरसते है जिस अपनेपन और प्यार के लिए।
वो हर भारतीय के घर में पाया जाता है।।

यँहा जैसा खाना नही कंही और मिल पाता है।
ना बाहर ऐसा पहनावा कंही और दिखता है।
अलग अलग प्रान्तो के बीच मे इतना प्यार।
सिर्फ मेरे भारत मे नज़र आता है।।
Title (writeup 2)
हिमालय हमारे भारत की पहचान

ऊंचा हिमालय देखो हिम का ताज पहने खड़ा है।
अपना ऊंचा मस्तक रख नभ से बाते कर रहा है।
ना डरता है ये कभी अपने रास्ते की बाधाओं से।
ये तो युगों युगों से हमारे भारत की पहचान बना है।।

ये मेघो को रोकने की ताकत अपने अंदर रखता है।
यह वीर की भांति आंधी से भी लड़ जाता हैं
ना कोई डर ना कोई भय ये तो अपने पग पर डट कर खड़ा है।

ये तो युगों युगों से हमारे भारत की पहचान बना है।।

चंदन जैसी सुगंध ये हमे प्रदान करता है।
झरने गाते गीत का आनंद हमे देता है।
हिमालय के दर्शन से मानो हम स्वर्ग पहुँच जाते है।
ये तो युगों युगों से हमारे भारत की पहचान बना है।।

ये ना कभी रास्तो में आने वाली बाधाओं से डरता है।
ये तो हमेशा रास्तो की बाधाओं से लड़ता है।
नही झुकाता अपना मस्तक कभी बाधाओं के आगे।
ये तो युगों युगों से हमारे भारत की पहचान बना है।।

रास्तो की रुकावटो से नही तुम्हे कभी डरना है।
सीना तानकर तुम्हे दुश्मन के आगे खड़ा होना है।
बस यही शिक्षा हमेशा हिमालय हमे देता है।
ये तो युगों युगों से हमारे भारत की पहचान बना है।।

Sahina Ghugha

Sahina Ghugha is 20 year old b.com student at Saurashtra university Rajkot. She is from Jamnagar city of Gujarat. She is state level winner in poetry competition 2017. She is Co-author of 10+ anthologies. She is an amazing writer and poet and she wants do something for society through her pen.

Insta ID:-
Itz_Sahina_write

हिन्दुस्तान

कहीं उछलता दरिया है
कहीं रेत सा रेगिस्तान।
कहीं पहाड़ों की वादियां
कहीं जंगल सा धान।

हर धर्म के लोग यहां
हर धर्म को देते मान।
इसलिए तो सबसे अच्छा
है मेरा हिंदुस्तान।

कहीं स्वाद रसगुल्ले का
कहीं सरसो दा साग ।
हो खमन ढोकला की खुश्बू
या हो कश्मीरी पान।

मंदिर मस्जिद एक लगे
है एक गीता कुरआन।
इसीलिए तो सबसे अच्छा
है मेरा हिंदुस्तान।

बाटे नहीं जाते मजहब यहां
सब लगते एक समान।
नाज़ होता है हिंद पे,
हिंद है हमारी शान।

लहराता तिरंगा ऊंचाइयों पे,
छू लेता है आसमान।
इसीलिए तो सबसे अच्छा
है मेरा हिंदुस्तान।

Sakshi Sharma

Ms. Sakshi Sharma belongs Aligarh, U.P. She like to decorate her words and emotions on paper and has participated in various anthologies as co-author. She is biotechnologist and researcher by profession with more than 2 years of experience. Additionally, she is national kathak dancer. She wants to be unique! To stand out amongst the people and like to learn new things. She believes in delivering smiles on the faces.

Indian Elegance!

A lot of traditions we follow in India,
the best is, we proud of colours in India,
Rajasthan is the beauty of palace,
as the women wears beautiful lehanga,
Gujarata has it's charming culture,
as women does dandia and garba,
dances we do, it is God's grace in India,
Kathak in UP, explains all the form of beauty,
Odissi has it's own culture of fascinating,
sangeet has it's own creativity,
whereas, dresses has it's wide popularity,
traditions and rituals in India,
we follow, we unite as the family of India,
Shakti is the soul of country,
whenever women hurts, India feels guilty,
That's why, proud all colours of India,
It's all about the pure souls in india,
beauty comes from heart,
and it's the colorful culture of India.

Beauty of India

The description of India's diversity is unique,
Everything here is unique,
There are mountains, churning of rivers,
there is the king of desert,
The township is here in Mayanagari,
every province here is very nice,
Amar Jawaan Jyoti, like Pride of India,
The valley of Kashmir reminds me of Darya,
Ganges water is cool, like nectar,
History creates, the walls of India,
Art resides in the soul, everyone here is virtuous,
Shakti is here settlement, devotion is also non-traditional,
The description of India's diversity is unique,
Everything here is unique,
Many stories settled here in every particle,
A new story for everyone here
This is India, Nirguna, Nirala,
Its beauty is fabulous,
Adopts everyone in the same bag,
This is India, our star, our pride,
The description of India's diversity is unique,
Everything here is unique.

Saroj Rana

She is Saroj Rana from Bharuch .She is do job at Amity School Bharuch from twenty six year.Her hobbies are reading and writing She completed M.A. in gujrati.She published her write up in anthology

સૈનિક છું.

પ્રકાર :- છંદોબદ્ધ રચના.(ગાગાલગા 4)
સાહસ ભરેલાં શૌર્યને, છલકાવતો સૈનિક છું,*
હુંકાર છે જુસ્સા ભરી,લલકારતો સૈનિક છું,

મરદાનગી રગરગ ભરી,કરવી રક્ષા સ્વદેશની,
વિશ્વાસથી આ શ્વાસને,મહેંકાવતો સૈનિક છું,

માભોમ કાજે તો મરી ફિટવાની ખેવના,
ઝાંસી તણી રાણી બની, લલકારતો સૈનિક છું,

નસનસ બહાદુરી ભરી, દુશ્મન ઘણાં હંફાવતો,
લડવૈયો થઇ દુશ્મન બધાં,ફટકારતો સૈનિક છું,

સમરંગણે લોહી વહે,પરવાહ ક્યારે ના કરું,
ઘા ઝીલવા તલવારનાં,પડકારતો સૈનિક છું,

શૂરાતને પાછો પડું,ડરપોક ક્યારે ના બનું,
હિંમત,પરાક્રમ,પ્રેમને,વખણાવતો સૈનિક છું,

સરહદ ભલે કાંટા ભરી,જુસ્સો હજી અકબંધ છે,
યોધ્ધા બની સંજોગને,પડકારતો સૈનિક છું,

*સરોજ રાણા..ભરચ.

Title (writeup 2)

શીર્ષક :- વતન.

પ્રકાર :- રજઝ છંદ.

બંધારણ :- ગાગાલગા 4.

ભારત ચમન છે પ્રેમનું,આ દેશ છે મારું વતન,
આઝાદ ભારત દેશનાં, સંતાનને પ્યારું વતન,

ધરતી શહીદોથી ભરી,યશગાન ગાયે માનથી,
જયાં શાન તિરંગા તણી, સચવાય શણગારું વતન,

કિસાન મારા દેશનો,તનતોડ શ્રમ કરનાર છે,
પુરુષાર્થની સોડમ વડે,મહેકાવશે ન્યારું વતન,

ઝંઝીર ગુલામી તણી, તોડી ગયાં ભડવીર સૌ,
આ માતૃભૂમિની રક્ષા કાજે ફના થાશું વતન,

રગરગ ભરી છે વીરતા,લૂંટાવશું સંગ્રામમાં,
સૈનિક બની સંભાળશું,બસ ના કદી હારું વતન,

સંસ્કાર છે આ દેશનાં, જેનું મને ગૌરવ વધુ,
જયાં એકતાને ભાઈચારાથી સહિયારું વતન,

*સરોજ રાણા...ભરુચ..20/4/21.

Shaimee Oza

She is shaimee oza from Mahesana.live in hostel in Ahemdabad.She write her write up with Nick name Lafz.She participated many anthology as co auther.She is costume designer.She is tantri in magazine.She got many trophies ,madals in literature.

ओह देशवासी तुम सदा सलामत रहोगे।
मां भारत की रक्षा के लिए ,
छोड़ दिया अपना परिवार किसीने देश के भरोसे।।
ओ देशवासी तुम मत बन इतना नराधम।
तेरी आजादी के लिए खून की नदिया बही है।।
किसी मां की काँख उज्जड गई।
किसी की मांग का सिंदूर मिट गया।।
किसी ने गवा दी पीता की छत्रछाया।
यह दिन है उनकी शहादत याद करने का।।
दो सो साल गुलाम रहे ब्रिटिश सरकार के।
आजादी के लिए खून बहाने वाले की मत गाओ सिर्फ
कहानी।।
पूछ लो सवाल अपने अंतर आत्मा से ।
क्या हम आजाद है अपने मन से?।।
एक दिन तिरंगा ऊपर लहराएगा।
दूसरे दिन कचरपेटी एवम पैरो तले पाया जाएगा।।
किसी मां ने शेर सा बेटा दिया दिल पर पत्थर रखकर।
किसी वीरांगना ने दिया जीवनसाथी अपने आंसू छिपाकर।।
इस परिवार की वेदना को तुम जरा समझो।
इसकी शहादत को दिल से याद कर लो।।
मां भारती को आपकी कमी बर्तेगी।
सारी जनता इतिहास के पन्नो में आपकी शहादत
के गीत गुनगुनाएगी।।
सदा ऊंचा रहे देश का सर यह प्रण निभाने।
दुश्मनों को मिला दिया मिट्टी में,दिया अहसास
हिंद के पानी का।।
देश की रक्षा के लिए दे दी शहादत।
मान लिया तिरंगे को अपना कफन।।
चले गए मां भारत के शरण में।
चैन की नींद ले पाई देश की जनता।।
रखवाली कर रहे थे शेर हमारे।
अमरत्व पा कर,देशप्रेम का पाठ पढ़ाकर।
छोड़ कर चले गए परिवार को देश के भरोसे।।

Shalini B .S.

Shalini.B.S is a literature student.Her writing style are about the real feeling,simple and understanding and joyful.She is writing in the pen name of TARA'.most of her works are based on real life she loves to listen music and interested in drawing and painting.

,Love To India

I love INDIA
My soul is for INDIA
My life is for INDIA
I live is for INDIA
I will die for INDIA
I am INDIA first
I am INDIA last
I will try my best
To be worthy son of INDIAN
I will fo my best

Shivani Joshi

She is Shivani M.R. Joshi. She is from Ahmedabad , Gujrat and 20yrs old. She's a teacher by profession and a student too. She started developing interest in writing during lockdown (19/5/2020) and slowly slowly started participating in anthologies and computation . dedicated to an mix.Currently she's working as a project manager in Priun publications and project head in sunshine. She had wrote several write up anthologies and it created a passion in herself and it's her dream to become a doctor in future.

तू ही मेरी जान,
तू ही मेरी आन,
तू ही मेरी संस्कृति ,
तू ही मेरा सम्मान,
तू ही मेरा अभिमान,
तू मेरा स्वाभिमान,
तू ही मेरी दुनिया ,
तू ही मेरा जहांन,
हम गर्व से कहते हैं
मेरा भारत महान|
जय हिंद

Shivangi Suman

She is Shiwangi suman ,She currently pursuing BBALLB and I a m 3 rd year student. She likes to watch stories which has great meaning inside it.

I Love My India,

India a land where culture meets , India a land where there is Unity in diversity,India is place where we workshop land ,A place where we found yoga were vedic parama found ,largest education hub at the back then, India was known as golden birds which were rich in culture and heritage ,where we treat people equally of different shapes and sizes where when someone is in pain we give them helping hand and don't run away, A place were different communities live Hindu , muslim ,sikh ,chirstans,parsi , Gujarati and many more ,where food changes from every corner whether it is Bengal rassgull,South Idli sambhar,gujrat 's Dhokla or Amritsari lassi were given to us . Sometimes we fight ,some times we hold grudges but when anyone needs us nah we are their to them , India is not just a place it's our identity where we belong ,It's our soil where our ashes get dump ,India is known for its bravery and courage ,we are not coward we are fighters we find for our country with blood and sweat , India were many leaders are born subash chandra bose ,Bhagat Singh ,Mahatama gandi ,India a place where we respect our mothers know matter how high we fly we are connected to our roots ,we are interlink with eachother and I am really proud That I live in that country where people are respected ,were we workship every human kind where we are together with love and compassion ,I know there will be many arguments and struggles but I know it will resolve and it will shine high .I love you India and I am proud to be Indian

India

India is place of love and happiness ,India is a place where we enjoy different foods with Same taste ,India is divided in caste colur and creed but still I am proud of it . Because it's our home we belong our identity is related to it we are related to it.I love you India keep shining high ...

Shraddha Rai

She is from the City of Lakes, Bhopal, Madhya Pradesh. She is a student studying in third year, pursuing B.Sc-B.Ed & belongs to a middle class family. Her hobby is gardening. She loved to write quotes, articles and poems. She share her write-ups through social media like Instagram s_ilent_killer27 and on YourQuote as Shraddha Rai. You can follow her, to reach her writings. She is a great dreamer & passionate for writing. She is kind and a little bit emotional too. She loved to spend time with family and friends. She had written 100+ anthologies as a co-author.

Love You India:-

Yes, I live in a country known as India and I am an Indian,
Where you are treated equal whether you are a Hindu, Muslim, Sikh or a Christian,
Where cast, creed, colour and gender doesn't matter,
Where only love survives and there is no place for hatred,

I live in India where fighters like Mahatma Gandhi, Subhash Chandra Bose and Bhagat Singh are born,
Who fought for attaining freedom every day and dawn,
This is the country where Ganga, Yamuna and Saraswati reside,
But these are not the rivers they are our God's as we have decide,

I reside in a country where mere animal such as cow is treated as a God,
Where a simple stone carving is worshipped as Lord,
Where people worship every wheather,
This is the country where everyone live like sisters and brothers,

I live in a country where our head bows down when we greet each other,
Where our respect comes first when we see others,
Where hard work runs everytime in our veins,
Where dependency is not accepted though there is a lot of pain,

Yes, I live in a country where a girl is exemplified with Durga and Saraswati,
Where Ram ,Sita and Shiva , Parvati are our biggest lovers,
Where a mere guest is regarded as God,
Where innocency survives in everyone's hearts,

Yes, my country is modern , but it did not leave it's tradition,
Where every person is free to choose his/her own ambition,
Where a soldier is even ready to sacrifice his life for the country,
Where everyone has a pure heart who lives in our heart,

Uniquely characterised in our India country,
Where intentions and hearts of our people are pure,
So come on, let's say , North, South, East or West ,
Our India will always remain the best.

Subhash Singh Ranjan

शुभाशीष रंजन जमालपुर {बिहार} से एक बेहतरीन कवि हैं। उन्हें SR36 के एक पेन नाम के साथ रोमांटिक और प्रेरक कविताएं / उद्धरण लिखने का शौक है।आप उनकी इंस्टाग्राम आई.डी. @ranjanshubhashishish और YourQuote आई.डी. Shubhashish Ranjan पर जाकर उनकी कविताओं/उद्धरण का एक मजा ले सकते हैं।शुभाशीष रंजन आपकी मांग पर भी कविताएं/उद्धरण लिख सकते है|

E-Mail:shubhashishishranjansr36@gmail.com

बलिदान

आज फिर सारे देश ने आसूं बहाया है
लिपटकर तिरंगे में फिर कोई वीर आया है
माँ-बाप की तो वो इकलौती संतान था|
अपने छोटी बहन का वो भईया, अभिमान था
उसकी पत्नी को लोग क्या कहकर समझायेंगे
सोचो उस बच्चे की हालत,
क्या कहकर उसे बहलायेंगे?
देखते ही देखते,कुछ पलों में
उसकी तो खुशहाल दुनिया उजड़ गई !
देश के लिए न जाने ऐसे ही,
कितनी जिंदगियां गुजर गईं !

सपूत

उन वीर सपूतों को मेरा सलाम,
जो देश के लिए हो गये कुर्बान,
देश आपकी सहादत चाहकर भी,
ना भूल पाया था,ना भूल पाएगा|
भविष्य में,जब भी याद किये जायेंगे योद्धा,
आपका नाम सबकी जुबान पर आएगा|
खुद की ख़ुशियाँ को एक तरफ रखकर,
आप देश का कर्ज चुकाते है,
जितनी आप कठोर परिश्रम करते,
क्या उसका 1प्रतिशत इनाम पाते है?

Vaibhavi Pandya

Vaibhavi Pandya from India she is persuing her bachelors degree in literature. She began writing from dec'19 and still the journey of her writing is going with the flow.

What If"

What If there was one religion named INDIAN?
Then there would be no religious bias, right?

What If there was no racism?
Then there would be no 'fair n lovely', right?

What If there was no sex discrimination?
Then all would be on same sight, right?

What If there was one religion and oneness (unity)?
Then there would have been less murdered & suicides on the name of love & religion, right?

What If everyone understood that a boy & a girl can be friends & brother-sister too?
Then there would be no trust issues, right?

What If everyone got real motivation & dreams?
Then no one would be unemployed, right?

What If these all come true?
Then India willbe seen in developed countries, right?

Vasenna Christian

Vanessa is a passionate writer who writes to create happiness through words.

Freedom in India

Freedom in India
Isn't really free;
We often pay a price
To keep our liberty.

Remember those we loved,
Who fought for us, and died;
And those we never knew
For whom others mourned and cried.

At home our "war" for freedom
Is sadly overdue;
We've let corruption stage
A sad and grievous coup.

No longer can we brush off
Dishonesty and greed,
Lust for wealth and power;
We can't, we won't concede.
Title (writeup 2)
*Continue.....

Complacency is weakness
Patriots can't afford;
We have to act on wrongs
That cannot be ignored.

We must give up some time,
Spent on other pleasures,
To restore America's freedom,
To keep America's treasures.

Money spent on trifles
Must now go to our cause:
Get rid of the offenders,
Constitutional outlaws.

Freedom in India
Isn't really free
It's up to American patriots;
It's up to you and me.

Zarana Raja

She is Zarana Raja from Bharuch.She write her write up with Nick name Zara.She write gazal,poem,microfiction ,story and now a days try to write a novel.Her hobbies are teach and learn something new everyday.

ગઝલ: એ દેશ ભારત છે

છંદ: હજઝ (લગાગાગા*4)

હિમાલય સરહદે કરતો નમન એ દેશ ભારત છે,
ચરણમાં સિંધુઓ કરતા વહન એ દેશ ભારત છે.

જ્યાં નાખો નજર દેખાય હરિયાળી બધે સુંદર,
સુમનથી શોભતા અઢળક ચમન એ દેશ ભારત છે.

જુદા પોશાક ભાષા પણ જુદી ne છે અલગ રીતો,
વિવિધ લોકનું બન્યું છે જે સદન એ દેશ ભારત છે.

દયા ને સ્નેહ સાથે રાખતી હિંમત બધી જનતા,
સદા જ્યાં પ્રેમ વરસાવે ગગન એ દેશ ભારત છે.

ગણિતનું જ્ઞાન ભારત પીરસે શૂન્ય દઈ જગને,
જે મબલક જ્ઞાનનું કરતું ચયન એ દેશ ભારત છે.

ઝરણા રાજા. "ઝારા

Flairs and Glairs, a platform by a student for the students. We are esteemed youth struggling to carve out our path for our future and we follow a basic mindset Since everyone is not born with all-round skills. Joining hands with people who are born to execute it with perfection is the best way to evolve. Self-Evolution is the need of the hour but, evolving as a community is what we strive for. The initiative as kickstarted by, Founder- Mr. Shubham Shah with the motive to utilize the skillset and talent of writing has now a team of 10+ people who are actively participating into newer forms of learning and discovering talents among youngsters. We Provide platform and services like Publishing opportunities, Open mics, Workshops, Hands-on training. Operating with Brand Name of Flairs and Glairs (Publication House), we offer the chance of elevating a passionate writer to an esteemed author With Brand name Teekhe Zasbaaat. We bring to you an opportunity to get accustomed with the Public Speaking and Presenting of Thoughts along with regular challenges to brush up your inking spirit. The newest initiative to extend our services we introduced in a new writing Platform- The Glittering Fables and Ink Over Tears.

We Choose to Fly Like A Falcon than to be

a Leg Pulling Crab.

To Know More: Infoline – 7781900870
Mail Us At-
flairsandglairs@gmail.com / info@flairsandglairs.in
Or Visit is at
www.flairsandglairs.com / www.flairsandglairs.in
Social Handles- @flairsandglairs @teekhezasbaaat

www.ingramcontent.com/pod-product-compliance
Ingram Content Group UK Ltd.
Pitfield, Milton Keynes, MK11 3LW, UK
UKHW022003190726
13853UKWH00004B/1713